"Over there," Joe shouted as the man popped up from between two parked cars and ran toward Frank. They definitely had him trapped this time.

But the man surprised them. A dozen feet from Frank, he veered over to the open wall of the parking garage behind the stairwell. Was he going to jump? Frank wondered. They followed him and saw that he had lowered himself onto the roof of the enclosed walkway, which was like a giant glass tube sticking out from the third floor of the garage.

"Can't let him get away like this," Joe muttered. Crouched on top of the curved roof of the walkway for balance, the man had nearly made it to the building across the street.

Joe hopped down onto the top of the glass walkway. He stayed low and went after the man, mimicking his crouch. But the curved glass was a lot more slippery than it looked.

Joe was almost halfway across when he froze for an instant. He looked down at the drop.

Then he lost his balance, and his feet slid out from under him.

Books in THE HARDY BOYS CASEFILES™ Series

Available from ARCHWAY Paperbacks

THE HARDY BOYS

CASEFILES™

NO. 114

CLEAN SWEEP

FRANKLIN W. DIXON

AN ARCHWAY PAPERBACK
Published by POCKET BOOKS
New York London Toronto Sydney Tokyo Singapore

This book is a work of fiction. Names, characters, places and
incidents are products of the author's imagination or are used
fictitiously. Any resemblance to actual events or locales or per-
sons, living or dead, is entirely coincidental.

AN ARCHWAY PAPERBACK *Original*

An Archway Paperback published by
POCKET BOOKS, a division of Simon & Schuster Inc.
1230 Avenue of the Americas, New York, NY 10020

Copyright © 1996 by Simon & Schuster Inc.
Produced by Mega-Books, Inc.

ISBN: 0-671-50456-8

First Archway Paperback printing August 1996

10 9 8 7 6 5 4 3 2 1

THE HARDY BOYS, AN ARCHWAY PAPERBACK
and colophon are registered trademarks of Simon & Schuster Inc.

THE HARDY BOYS CASEFILES is a trademark
of Simon & Schuster Inc.

Cover photograph from "The Hardy Boys" Series © 1995 Nelvana
Limited/Marathon Productions S.A. All rights reserved.

Logo design TM & © 1995 by Nelvana Limited. All rights reserved.

Printed in the U.S.A.

IL 6+

CLEAN SWEEP

Chapter

1

"I CAN'T BELIEVE THIS," Frank Hardy grumbled as he studied the map spread out on the dashboard. "We're lost. And we're so late, Richie probably thinks we're not coming."

"So what?" said Frank's younger brother, Joe. "After all the practical jokes he's played on us, he'll figure we're just trying to get even by not showing up."

Joe was behind the wheel of the black van the brothers shared. Instead of cruising on an interstate, they were bouncing down a narrow dirt road that Joe had insisted would cut half an hour off their trip. Joe wrenched the wheel from one side to the other, trying to avoid the many potholes.

1

"Joe, I'm telling you," Frank said, "if we just head north we'll eventually hit I-77 again. Then we can get our bearings and—"

"And tack an extra hour onto the trip," Joe said. "No, thanks. My gut tells me we're going in the right direction. And since I'm driving, my gut beats your map."

Frank sighed as he stared out the passenger-side window at a field full of grazing cows. He and Joe were on their way to Langston University to help their friend Richie Simmons move back to school for his sophomore year. An hour earlier their route had been blocked by an accident. Rather than wait for it to be cleared, Joe had decided to take off on this dirt road.

Leave it to Joe, Frank thought, to jump first and ask questions later. He just didn't believe in reason or logic, relying instead on his instincts. Frank had to admit, though, that Joe's recklessness often did get results.

Joe coaxed the van up a hill and broke into a grin as the interstate came into view. "See, I was right," he said, slapping his brother on the back. In a few minutes they were back on the highway, roaring past a sign that read Exit 9, Langston University, 14 miles.

"I told you my gut would get us here," Joe said.

"Your gut got lucky," Frank said. He threw

the road map into the back of the van, among the boxes and milk crates filled with Richie's belongings.

Richie had been in Frank's class at Bayport High, where Frank was a senior and Joe a junior, but Richie had managed to graduate two years early. Considering Richie's talent for driving everyone crazy with practical jokes and pranks, Frank figured the teachers let him graduate early just to get him out of their hair.

Half an hour later Frank and Joe arrived at Richie's dorm, a modern brick building surrounded by trucks and cars pulling trailers, all piled high with boxes and luggage. Joe parked the van, and he and Frank jumped out. A redheaded girl in a Langston University sleeveless top jogged by and smiled at Joe.

"I think I'm going to like it here," he said.

"Yeah, well, we're here to help Richie, not to go sightseeing," Frank said with a chuckle.

They made their way past a pair of students balancing a huge carton loaded with books and climbed the stairs to the third floor. The hallway was deserted.

Joe checked the numbers on the doors. "Three-seventeen must be this way," he said.

Frank followed his brother, wondering why this floor was so dead. They reached room 317 and rapped on the door.

"Hello, Mr. Simmons," he yelled. "The Hardy Brothers Moving Company is here with your junk."

No answer.

Joe frowned. "Maybe he went out to look for us."

The door across the hall from Richie's opened a crack, and both brothers spun around. Frank went over and tried to peer inside, but the room was pitch dark.

"What's going on out there?" someone shouted.

"We're looking for Richie Simmons," Frank said, stepping back from the door. "Do you know him?"

"Yeah, I know him," the voice said. "He told me you might stop by. He said if I saw you to give you ... this!"

The plastic barrel of a huge pump-action water gun appeared around the edge of the door and blasted Frank with a stream of icy water.

Suddenly doors up and down the hall flew open. At least ten guys jumped out wielding water guns and softball-size water balloons.

"Open fire!"

Frank turned and saw Richie Simmons twirling a pair of water pistols like a gunfighter from an old Hollywood western.

"Let's see if they can dance, boys," Richie drawled. He fired both guns at Frank's feet.

4

A water balloon came sailing toward Frank, who ducked just in time for it to nail Richie in the chest.

"I'm hit!" Richie yelled, still firing away with both water pistols.

The guy who had thrown the water balloon snatched another one from a plastic laundry basket filled with them. Joe charged, bellowing like a bull with a matador in his sights. The next water balloon hit Joe square in the chest, but it didn't slow him down. As the water bomber scrambled for more ammo, Joe snatched the basketful of balloons and slid it down the hallway to Frank.

"Way to go, Bob," Richie said to the water bomber. "Why didn't you just roll out the fire hose for them? If I—"

Frank hurled a balloon. Richie tried to dodge it, but the water splattered across his back. Joe skidded over to join his brother, and the two of them started lobbing balloons as fast as they could.

The ambushers ducked behind the doors for cover. Frank and Joe spent the rest of their ammo slamming the balloons against the doors. By the time they ran out, every inch of the floor was drenched.

Richie finally emerged from a room with his hands raised over his head.

"Okay, I surrender," he said. "Now I know

how Napoleon felt at Waterloo. Hey, what took you guys so long anyway? Did you go to the wrong university?"

When Frank and Joe started to tell Richie their separate versions of how they got lost, some of Richie's friends figured out that they could slide twenty or thirty feet on the wet linoleum floor if they got a good running start. Joe liked what he saw and decided to try it.

"Does this kind of stuff go on a lot?" Frank asked.

"What kind of stuff?" Richie asked.

Joe went zipping past them, throwing up a spray of water.

"Turning the hallway into a water park."

"It calms down a little when classes start," Richie said, grinning. "The university assigns a resident assistant to every floor, a graduate student who keeps an eye on us."

"So where's your resident assistant?" Frank asked.

"That's him in the red shirt," Richie said, pointing at a guy trying to slide like a bowling ball into some of the others. "Just kidding. Actually, we have him tied up in the laundry room."

"He must be gagged, too," Frank said, "because I don't hear him yelling for help."

"Okay, okay," Richie said. "If we must be serious, he's at some kind of resident assistant training—probably learning what to do when the guys on the floor go berserk and turn it into a water park."

Joe came sliding toward them and grabbed Frank to stop. "Come on," he told his brother. "You've got to try this."

Richie put his hands on his hips and slipped into his best impression of Ms. Dominic, the head of Bayport High School's history department. "Is that all you two ever think about—having fun?" he said in Ms. Dominic's stern nasal twang. "That van's not going to unload itself, boys. You know that. Now, come on, let's get to work."

Frank rolled his eyes. Same old Richie.

They spent a few minutes mopping up the hallway. When all the towels they could find were soaked through, they went downstairs to start unloading. Frank backed the van up to the stairwell closest to Richie's room, and they all loaded up with boxes and milk crates and started upstairs.

Frank took a look at the mess in the crate he was carrying. "It looks like you just emptied your desk drawers in here, Richie," he said.

"That's exactly what I did. It only took me half an hour to pack. That's about how long it'll take me to unpack, too. I just dump the stuff back into my drawers."

7

When they reached Richie's floor, the rest of the guys from the ambush had finished mopping up and were snapping the wet towels at one another. Richie led the way to his room, where he dropped his boxes on his side of the room. Open boxes and half-unpacked suitcases cluttered the other side.

"So which one of those guys is your roommate?" Joe asked.

"None of them. He went out to run some errands."

Joe looked at some of the books stacked on the other bed. Most of them had to do with environmental issues. "What's he like?"

Richie shrugged. "I just met him this morning. His name's Eli Travers. He transferred this year from Amberlin College. He likes my video game selection, I like his CD collection. We should get along pretty well."

"Does he mind that we're camping out on your floor tonight?" Frank asked.

"No. He's looking forward to meeting you. If he gets back in time, I'm going to show all three of you around."

It took them only a half dozen more trips to empty the van. Richie's roommate wasn't back yet, but they decided to go explore the campus anyway.

"So where to first?" Richie said.

"Where do you hang out?" Joe asked. "You know—someplace with music, food, girls."

They left the dorm and started down the sidewalk, which was lined with stately oak and maple trees.

"I think I know just the place. . . ." Richie said with a grin. "Hey, there's Eli." Richie pointed to a big guy with red hair waving at them from about a block away.

As they approached Eli, a beat-up green van with a cracked windshield pulled up beside him. When the driver leaned out to say something to Eli, Frank saw he was wearing a gorilla mask. "Who's that?" he asked.

"You mean *what's* that?" Richie said. "Maybe he needs directions to the zoo."

Eli started to walk away from the van, but the driver leaped out and grabbed the front of Eli's T-shirt.

"Hey, that gorilla's got a gun," Frank shouted.

Eli tried to pull away, but the masked man pointed the gun at his head and shoved him into the van through the driver's door.

"Let's get him," Frank said as he started to sprint toward the van.

Joe took off after his brother. Then the driver, who was back in the van, leaned out his window, took aim, and fired three quick shots at the Hardys.

9

Chapter

2

AT THE SOUND of the shots, Frank and Joe ducked behind a car. They heard several panicked shouts, and Frank glanced all around them. As far as he could tell, no one had been hit.

Joe got up and raced down the sidewalk toward the van, Frank charging after him.

The van's engine roared, drowning out any shouts. Joe was desperate to grab on to the van, but it was already moving too fast.

"Watch it," Frank shouted as the van turned and swerved toward them.

The younger Hardy dove over the trunk of a parked sedan just as the van plowed into it with a grinding shriek of metal on metal.

Frank ducked around the sedan and lunged for the rear of the van as it pulled away. It was accelerating fast, but he managed to grab the back door handles and climb up onto the bumper.

Through the back window Frank could see Eli sitting on a spare tire against the left wall only a few feet away.

Frank hung on to the left-hand door, struggling to keep his balance, while he pulled the right one open.

"Let's go," Frank yelled.

"I can't," Eli said. "I'm handcuffed."

The driver glanced in the rearview mirror, angled his right arm around to point the automatic, and fired two more shots.

Frank ducked behind the door as the first shot shattered the window just above his head, sending glass fragments flying off the back of the van.

The door flew open, and Frank had to hoist himself up to grab on to the top of the door or he would have been dragged along the asphalt. He figured the van was going forty miles an hour by now.

Behind the van was a red convertible with its top down. The driver was a blond girl in sunglasses, who was staring open-mouthed at Frank.

Frank had to make a move. If he didn't, he

was either going to get shot or fall off and be run over.

Because the man in the gorilla mask had to slow the van to take aim again, the convertible pulled up closer. Frank saw his chance. He planted his feet on the bumper and pushed off backward, spinning in the air and landing spread-eagled on the hood of the convertible. The impact knocked the breath out of him, but he managed to stay on.

The convertible braked to a stop, and Frank sat up to watch the van pull away. Just before it disappeared around a corner, he noticed it had no license plate. He could hear sirens in the distance, but he figured they were probably too far away to catch the van.

The driver of the convertible slid her sunglasses down her nose and studied Frank.

"That's a funny way to hitch a ride," she said. "Is this some kind of fraternity prank?"

Frank shook his head, slid off the hood, and came around to the driver's side. "Hi, I'm Frank Hardy," he said, sticking out his hand.

"Nice to meet you, Frank, I'm Sylvia," the driver said, shaking Frank's hand. "Why don't you hop in? I'll give you a ride, and you can explain all this. You can understand why I'd be kind of curious."

Frank gave her directions back to Richie's dorm and, on the way, told her about Eli being kidnapped. She dropped him off out front, where two police cars were parked, their lights flashing. One officer was talking to a guy with dreadlocks who seemed to be the owner of the sedan with the banged-up fender. Another officer was interviewing Richie and Joe, who broke away when he saw Frank coming.

"And you call *me* reckless!" Joe said. "What happened?"

Frank told them about his wild ride on the back of the van. Then one of the officers asked Richie and the Hardys to come down to the station to file a report.

As Frank slid into the back of the squad car with Richie and Joe, he noticed his brother was carrying a shopping bag.

"What's that, Joe?" he asked.

"Eli dropped it at the kidnap scene, and I picked it up."

"Nice going," Franks said. "Did you check inside?"

"It's just a bunch of textbooks," Joe said. He pulled out the books and shuffled through them. "Organic chemistry, environmental science, microbiology. This guy is going for a major brain overload."

Frank turned to Richie. "What else do you know about Eli?"

"Not much. I just met him a few hours ago, remember? We could ask some of the other guys on the floor. Eli got there yesterday and hung out with them last night."

Joe was leafing through one of the textbooks. He paused to sound out one of the longest words he'd ever seen in the English language. "Trichlorophenoxyacetic acid."

"What is that?" Richie asked.

"Beats me, but the book says the Environmental Protection Agency banned it in the seventies. Probably because no one could pronounce it."

As Joe continued to flip through the book, a folded piece of paper fell out.

Frank picked the paper up off the floor of the car. It was a photocopied flyer promoting the Student Action Committee's fall organizing meeting next week.

"What do you know about the S.A.C.?" Joe asked.

"It's one of those activist groups," Richie said. "I remember them staging a protest last year against experimenting on animals. Eli is an environmental science major, so it makes sense that he'd be interested in the committee."

Frank waved the flyer. "Where do you think he picked this up?"

"The Union Mall, probably," Richie said.

"That's funny," Joe said. "He didn't look

like the kind of guy you'd see hanging out at a mall."

"It's not a shopping mall," Richie explained. "It's the main lawn of the campus. Kids hang out there, play Frisbee, study, whatever. This time of year, a lot of clubs set up information booths there to recruit new members. I'm sure the S.A.C. has one."

"That'd be worth checking out," Frank said. "Eli may have talked to somebody there."

Richie looked back and forth between the brothers. "So you two are going to do your detective bit? Be the heroes and help me find my missing roommate?"

The Hardys looked at him.

"What do you think?" Joe asked.

"I think you're going to, because I think you can't help it," he said.

When they arrived at the police station, Detective Loomis, a stout, balding man with a businesslike manner, met them and led them to a cluttered desk. A couple of half-empty foam coffee cups were balanced on its edge. He started right in with questions about the kidnapping, shoving enough of the mess over to fill out a form.

As Frank gave Detective Loomis his statement, Joe checked out the open office area. There was a lot of activity; both county sheriff's deputies and state police were there. There were also plenty of men in suits. They'd be FBI, Joe decided. The agency had to be called in on any kidnapping. But there must be something else big going on, Joe thought, because it was too soon for Eli's kidnapping to have drawn all this attention.

Within ten minutes Loomis was finished taking Frank's statement.

"What's going on?" Joe asked the detective. "It looks like you've got every agency in the state here. Is it some kind of law enforcement convention or something?"

Loomis frowned at him. "Nothing special. Just a regular meeting about interagency cooperation." Then he took statements from Joe and Richie.

The office area began to clear out, and one of the other detectives walked by and said, "Time to wrap it up, Loomis. The meeting's about to start."

"Okay, fellows," Detective Loomis said, standing up and reaching out to shake hands all around. "You know where to reach me if anything else turns up." Richie and the Hardys said their goodbyes and headed for the exit.

"If that's a regular meeting, I'm a Girl Scout," Joe muttered to his brother.

"You're right," Frank said. "Something's up,

but I doubt it has anything to do with Eli. They couldn't have mobilized that fast."

"Maybe somebody will let us in on the big secret," Richie said.

As they reached the double glass doors at the main entrance, they heard a voice calling out, "Hey, Frank and Joe Hardy! Wait a second."

They turned and saw a uniformed city police officer hurrying toward them. He was tall, slim, dark-haired, and not much older than they were.

"Sorry, Officer," Frank said, "but do we know you?"

He laughed and hooked his thumbs in his belt. "No, probably not. My name's Mike De-Finis. My dad's a police detective in New York. He used to know your dad when they were on the force together years ago."

Frank and Joe remembered their father's stories about working in the New York Police Department before he became one of the most successful and respected private investigators in the business.

"Laughing Lou DeFinis," Joe said. "Of course. We've heard Dad talk about him."

"Right," DeFinis said. "And I've heard a lot about you guys from my dad. Anyway, my buddy Paul was one of the officers on the scene of your friend's kidnapping. He told me all about it. I just wanted to say hello and see if there's anything I can do to help."

"Thanks," Frank said. "What's with the convention in there, anyway?"

"Have you heard of General Sean Albright?"

"Sure," Frank said. He had read about Albright, a recently retired four-star army general. "He does special diplomatic missions for the State Department."

"That's the guy," DeFinis said. "He's a Langston University alumnus, and he's going to be on campus for a few days. The meeting's about security for his visit. I heard there may be some protests while he's here. I should be getting back in there now. Here's my phone number. Let's stay in touch. I'd like to help you guys find your friend."

After Richie gave Officer DeFinis his phone number, they thanked him and headed back to the dorm.

Frank and Joe, eager to get cracking, spent a restless night on the floor of Richie's room. By nine o'clock the next morning, the three had already had breakfast and were heading across the Union Mall. Students were scattered all over the big grassy lawn, strumming guitars, juggling, playing catch, and just soaking up the late August sunshine.

A couple of dozen booths lined the sidewalks that crisscrossed the mall.

"There's the S.A.C. banner," Joe said, leading Frank and Richie over. Several students were manning the booth, which was plastered with newspaper articles about political and environmental issues.

A girl in a tie-dyed dress greeted them. "Are you three interested in helping us make Langston University—and the world—a better place to live?" she asked.

"We sure are," Joe said. "But first we're hoping you can help us track down a friend of ours who might have stopped by here yesterday."

He described Eli, and the girl nodded. "Sure I remember him," she said. "Jessica talked to him for ten or fifteen minutes. She said she was pretty sure he was going to join."

"Great," Frank said. "Is Jessica here?"

"No. But you can find her at our office in the Student Union, room three-oh-seven." She pointed at a long brick building with a gabled roof at one end of the mall.

They thanked her and headed for the Student Union. Richie took them in a side entrance and up two flights of stairs to room 307. The door was open, and as they approached, they could hear raised voices inside.

"Just get out," said a woman's voice.

Inside the office a young blond woman in a S.A.C. T-shirt was holding up a clipboard and a phone and pointing them at two questionable-looking characters.

One of them, unshaven and with a scraggly brown ponytail, was perched on the edge of a long table covered with photocopied flyers.

"Get out now or I'll call the police," the woman said.

The other guy, big and beefy with a shaved head, was leaning over the phone cord. "Not on this phone, you won't," he said, grabbing the cord in one hand and ripping it out of the wall with a sharp yank.

"I said get out," the girl said.

The beefy, bald guy straightened up and laughed. "Now, who's going to make us?"

Joe stepped up and said, "That would be us, Curly."

Frank stood shoulder to shoulder with his brother as the two troublemakers turned to face them.

The big one chuckled and started toward Joe. "Watch how you talk to me, Blondie."

Frank stepped between them and held up his hands. "All right," Frank said. "Let's try to settle this before someone gets hurt."

The big thug stared down at Frank. "Forget it, punk," he said. Then he reared back, cocked his fist, and swung a right hook at Frank's jaw.

Chapter

3

FRANK DUCKED under the bald guy's punch, grabbed one massive arm with both hands, and flipped him out the door, sending him crashing into the opposite wall of the hallway.

"Ouch," Richie said. "Too bad he didn't have any hair to cushion the impact."

The smaller troublemaker glared at the Hardys with narrowed eyes. His big partner got up and loomed in the doorway, flushed and breathing heavily. "I'm gonna crush you," he said to Frank.

Richie scooted around the edge of the room and took a seat by the table. "This should be good," he said to the blond girl. "Frank there, he's competed in the state karate championships three times and brought back the gold every time. Joe, on the other hand, is more of a scrapper. He just pounds and pounds until the other guy goes down. Nothing can stop him."

"Yeah, right," the huge guy muttered.

The guy with the ponytail threw a glance over his shoulder at Richie. Then he slipped a hand inside his denim jacket.

"Watch it," Joe said, figuring he was going for a weapon.

Ponytail stepped back a few inches and slowly pulled his hand from his jacket. It was empty.

Not a bad bluff, Joe thought.

Meanwhile, the blond girl slipped behind the desk in the corner, picked up a video camera from the floor, and started taping. She narrated crisply for the camera. "We're in the S.A.C. office. J. J. Nye and Dale Shapley are trespassing. They've already ripped the phone cord out of the wall and assaulted the three people who came to my rescue. If they don't get out of here now, this tape is going to the police as evidence."

"Not if we take it first," said the huge guy. He and his partner moved in on her, but Frank and Joe stepped in front of them.

"You asked for it," the big guy said to Joe, cocking his fist again.

"Don't do it, Dale," Ponytail said. "With

22

your record, if they get you on tape throwing the first punch you're going to do serious time."

The big guy hesitated. "All right, but I better not catch any of you three nosing around us anymore," he said, jabbing his finger at Joe, Frank, and Richie, one by one, "because if I do, you'll be sorry."

"It was nice to meet you, too," Joe said as the two turned and walked out the door.

"Thanks for the buildup, Richie," Frank said. "But just for future reference, they don't give out gold medals at karate tournaments."

Richie shrugged. "Those two geniuses didn't know that. And, hey, at least it got their attention."

Joe stepped out in the hall to make sure the two thugs were really leaving. The only other person he saw was a man carrying an umbrella and wearing a tweed sport jacket, blue jeans, and white tennis shoes. He looked too old to be a student, so Joe figured he must be a professor.

The girl set the camera on the desk, brushed her bangs out of her eyes, and let out a sigh.

Frank asked, "Who were those guys?"

"The big one is Dale Shapley," she said. "The other is J. J. Nye. They used to be students here, but they were kicked out for setting a professor's car on fire. They like to think

THE HARDY BOYS CASEFILES

of themselves as activists, but they don't really care about anything. They just use legitimate causes as an excuse for vandalism.''

"What were they doing here?" Frank asked.

"They've got it in for me because I testified against them as an eyewitness when they torched the car. They not only got expelled from the university but also had to do community service.''

"That was the 'record' one of them referred to?" Joe said.

"Part of it. Shapley was also arrested for beating up some guy last year," she said. "He served thirty days in jail. But enough about those two losers. Are you guys here to sign up? We really could use your help.''

"Sorry," Joe said, "but we're not students.''

Frank introduced himself, Joe, and Richie and said, "We're looking for Jessica.''

"That's me.''

"Richie's roommate was kidnapped yesterday," Joe said. "His name is Eli Travers.''

Jessica went pale and plopped down into her desk chair. "Eli was kidnapped?" she said. "Are you sure?''

Frank and Joe told her about the green van, the man in the gorilla mask, and how Eli had been shoved inside and handcuffed. She shook her head in disbelief. The news seemed to hit her hard.

"We heard you were talking to Eli yesterday at the booth on the mall," Frank said. "Did you know him well?"

She didn't answer at first. "Not really," she finally said. "I just met him. He said he was a transfer student—from Amberlin College, I think. It's just bizarre, finding out he was kidnapped right after I talked to him."

"Did he say anything about where he had been or where he was going?" Frank asked.

She stopped to think. "Yes. He said a professor he knew from Amberlin was going to be teaching here this year, and Eli was going to look him up."

"Excellent," Joe said. "Do you remember the professor's name?"

She shook her head. "No. Sorry. I don't think Eli mentioned it. He did say 'him,' though, so at least we know it's a man."

"Did he mention what subject the professor teaches?" Frank asked.

"Some kind of science, I think, from the way Eli was talking."

"That's something," Frank said. "Can you think of anything else he said that might help us find him?"

Jessica chewed her lower lip. "Nothing that he said, but those two guys you chased out of here, Nye and Shapley . . . After Eli left the S.A.C. booth, I saw him talking to them."

"Do you think they'd kidnap him?" Joe asked.

"I don't know. I can't imagine why, unless it was just a vicious prank."

"Do you know where we can find them?" Frank asked.

"Sure. They rent a house off campus, but you'll probably find them up at the incinerator site, where we're staging a protest. They'll probably be there."

"What's the incinerator site?" Joe asked.

"The military is building a facility about twenty miles from here. It's for disposing of chemical weapons," Jessica explained.

"They're going to be burning chemical weapons?" Joe asked. "What does that do to the atmosphere?"

"It's not a problem, according to the government," Jessica said, "but of course that's based on research conducted by and for the military. Anyway, the big danger comes from transporting the stuff. It's stockpiled at depots around the country. Instead of building an incinerator at each depot, they're taking the cheap route—building just one and then transporting all the chemicals to the one incinerator."

Frank nodded. "If there's any kind of accident en route it's going to be a major disaster."

"That's right. We're talking about some very

lethal chemicals here," Jessica said. "For example the VX nerve agent."

"Which is listed in the *Guinness Book of World Records* as the world's deadliest substance," Richie piped up.

"I thought that was banned a long time ago," Frank said.

"It was," Jessica said. "It's not manufactured anymore, but tons of the stuff have been sitting around in military depots for decades while the government decided what to do with it. And a lot of it is in these old, leaky M-55 rockets. Can you imagine convoys of trucks filled with that stuff driving here cross-country?"

"It's a big risk," Joe said.

"That's exactly what we're trying to tell people," Jessica said. "But it's hard to get their attention. A lot of people who live around here are against the incinerator, but we need to send a message to a wider audience. That's why we're so busy even though school hasn't started yet. We need to take advantage of General Albright's visit to stir up some media coverage."

She picked up one of the photocopied pages and handed it to Frank. "Here's a map showing how to get to the site. As I said, you'll probably find Nye and Shapley there. Believe it or not, some kids actually think they're cool."

Frank and Joe thanked Jessica for her help and gave her Richie's phone number in case she thought of anything else. Then the three of them went down to a cafeteria in the Union to plan their next move over chocolate malteds and a few plates of onion rings.

Joe was idly glancing around the cafeteria as they talked. He noticed the same man in the tweed jacket and jeans he'd seen in the upstairs hallway. He was reading a newspaper in a booth and sipping coffee. Joe wondered why the man needed an umbrella on such a nice day.

As soon as they polished off the onion rings, Richie said, "Do you think you can get along without me for a couple of hours? I've got to go stand in line to register for classes."

"No problem," Frank said. "Just tell us how to get to the School of Science. We're going to go see if we can find Eli's professor friend from Amberlin."

Richie gave them directions and said he'd meet them back at his room later.

Frank and Joe left the Student Union and headed out across the mall. The sidewalks were crowded with students now, most of them dressed in shorts and T-shirts and wearing backpacks.

"Heads up!" someone yelled. Joe spun around just in time to see a football spiraling down on a collision course for his head. He jumped up, snatched it out of the air with both hands, and cradled it under his left arm. Most of the people around him ducked.

"Nice catch," called the guy who had thrown the ball. Joe tossed it back to him, twenty-five yards in a tight spiral. Just then he noticed the man with the tweed jacket and umbrella a dozen yards behind them. As Joe glanced at him, the man looked away quickly and stepped up to the scuba club booth.

"That guy's following us," Joe said.

"Are you sure?" Frank said.

"Positive. This is the third time I've seen him in the last hour."

Frank shrugged. "So let's go talk to him."

As the Hardys approached, the man saw them and trotted off across the mall.

"Let's go," Joe said.

They had to weave in and out of groups of students and even jump over a few sprawling forms to keep up. When the man reached the far side of the mall, he raced across the street into an open-sided parking garage four levels high.

"Watch it!" Frank said as Joe nearly ran out in front of a delivery truck. As soon as the truck passed, Joe darted across the street and

29

into the parking garage. They could hear the man's footsteps echoing up the winding ramp. Joe bolted after him.

Frank headed for the stairwell in the corner and went up to the second level. He poked his head out and saw Joe running up the ramp.

Frank climbed to the third floor, where a glass-enclosed walkway spanned the busy street below. The walkway connected the garage to the university library. Seeing no sign of the man, Frank went up to level four, the roof, and waited.

Now he and Joe had the man trapped between them. Or so he thought. A minute later Joe came jogging up the ramp at the opposite end of the roof. He was surprised to see Frank standing there all alone.

They started toward each other.

"Over there," Joe shouted as the man popped up from between two parked cars and ran toward Frank. They definitely had him trapped this time.

But the man surprised them. A dozen feet from Frank, he veered over to the open wall behind the stairwell. Was he going to jump? Frank wondered. They followed him and saw that he had lowered himself onto the roof of the enclosed walkway, which was like a giant glass tube sticking out from the third floor of the garage.

"Can't let him get away like this," Joe muttered. Crouched on top of the curved roof of the walkway for balance, the man had nearly made it to the library building across the street.

Joe hopped down onto the top of the glass walkway. He stayed low and went after the man, mimicking his crouch. But the curved glass was a lot more slippery than it looked.

Joe was almost halfway across when he froze for an instant and made the mistake of looking down from the two-story drop. He lost his balance, and his feet slid out from under him.

Chapter
4

JOE LANDED FACEDOWN on top of the walkway and began to slide toward the edge. Another foot or two and he would fall two stories into traffic.

"Hang on, Joe," Frank yelled as he lowered himself onto the walkway and crawled toward his brother.

Joe had his hands pressed flat against the glass, but he was slipping fast. Both his feet were already dangling over the edge.

Frank was still ten feet away when Joe finally lost his grip. Frank lunged and made a grab for Joe's wrists, throwing his body to the opposite side of the glass tube from Joe. He caught one of Joe's hands and managed to hang on.

Now two pairs of legs were dangling, one on either side of the rounded glass dome covering the walkway. Frank's weight counterbalancing Joe's was the only thing that kept both of them from sliding off.

"Where's your other hand?" Frank asked.

Frank's face was pressed against the curved glass, and he saw a pair of students inside the walkway looking up at them in total shock.

"Here," Joe said, slapping the glass. Frank found it, and they got a better grip on each other.

"Okay. Now, careful," Frank said, "or else we both go over the edge."

"Right," Joe said. "On the count of three. One . . . two . . . three—"

They both swung their feet onto the glass, counterbalancing their weight and walked their way up. As soon as they met at the top, Joe started toward the library—this time on his hands and knees.

"What are you doing?" Frank said.

"Going forward's as easy as going back," Joe said. "Besides, we might still have a chance to catch that guy."

Frank followed his brother to the far side, where they pulled themselves up onto the roof and jogged over to a pair of gray fire doors. Joe pulled one of the handles. The door opened an inch and then stopped. He put his eyes to the crack and looked inside.

"He slid his umbrella through the handles," he said. "Grab the other door."

With both of them yanking hard, they managed to bend the umbrella enough to reach inside the doors and pull it out. They went down the stairs and found themselves on the top floor of the library, where shelves of books stretched as far as they could see. They split up to search for the man in the tweed jacket. After almost twenty minutes of looking through the stacks and reading rooms, they gave up and decided to head over to the School of Science.

Once they got there, they followed signs to the reception area on the first floor. All the classrooms and lecture halls along the corridor were empty.

Lights were on in the reception area, and there was a cup of steaming coffee on the desk, but no one was around. Beyond the reception area there were several offices and a workroom with a photocopier. Five large white boxes were stacked next to the reception desk.

Frank was about to call out to see if anyone was around when a loud crash sounded from inside one of the offices.

Frank and Joe rushed to the office door and found a woman with curly gray hair standing with her hands on her hips over an identical white box. Its contents—books, papers, and office supplies—were spilled out across the burgundy carpet.

She smiled sheepishly when she saw Frank and Joe. "I thought I could manage this box, but it was too heavy," she explained.

"We can help," Joe offered.

"Why, thank you," she said as the Hardys flipped the box upright and began to refill it.

"Are you moving to a different office?" Frank asked.

"Dear me, no," she said. "This was Dean Martinez's office. He was killed in an automobile accident last week. These are his personal effects."

"Oh," Frank said. "I'm sorry."

Joe lifted the box from the bottom, carried it to the outer office, and stacked it with the others. Frank noticed more boxes lined up beneath the empty bookshelves in the office.

"Would you like help with those boxes, too?" he asked.

"That would be lovely, thank you," the woman said. "I'm so lucky you boys happened along."

"Actually, we're here for a reason," Frank said. He hefted the first box and staggered a few steps, trying to keep his balance. The box

35

felt as if it were full of bricks. "We were hoping you could help us locate a professor."

He passed Joe in the doorway to the outer office. Joe grinned when he saw Frank struggling with the box. Frank stacked the box in the outer office and went back for another. He watched as Joe hauled out the next one, straining with the effort, and Frank chuckled.

"Who are you looking for?" the woman asked Frank. She was perched on the edge of the desk, watching the Hardys work.

"We don't know his name," Frank said, "but we're pretty sure he's in the School of Science. He's from Amberlin College."

"Oh, you must mean Professor Rocco," she said. "Such a nice man. There was another young man here yesterday looking for him."

Frank described Eli to her.

"Yes, that was him. Professor Rocco is over in the geology building. I looked up his office number for the young man yesterday. It's three twenty-four; I remember it because that's my birthday—March twenty-fourth."

Joe came back into the dean's office, flexing his shoulders and arms. He and Frank moved the last two boxes and then got directions to the geology building from the woman, who thanked them and waved as they left.

"Did she remind you of anybody?" Joe asked as they walked away.

"I don't know," Frank said. "Who do you think?"

"Aunt Gertrude," Joe said. "You know, the way she gets us to till her garden every spring while she sits in the shade and points out all the spots we missed."

"It'll be worth a few sore muscles in the morning," Frank said, "if Professor Rocco can shed some light on why anyone would want to kidnap Eli."

They found Professor Rocco in his office, highlighting passages in a textbook. He was a man of medium size and build in his mid-thirties, with a trim black mustache and a welcoming smile.

"Come in, come in," he said when he saw them in the doorway. "May I help you with anything? Are you interested in signing up for my environmental science course?"

"Well, not exactly," Frank said. "We're worried about Eli Travers."

"Ah, yes, Eli," he said. "You're friends of his?"

"Friends of a friend," Joe said. "Eli was kidnapped yesterday, and we're trying to find out why. Since you knew him at Amberlin, we figured you might be able to help."

"Kidnapped?" the man asked, shaking his

head. "Well, how in the world did that happen? Why?"

The Hardys filled the professor in on Eli's abduction. He seemed completely baffled by the whole situation.

"He came here to see you yesterday, didn't he?" Frank asked.

"Yes, yesterday afternoon," Rocco said.

"Did he give you any indication that he might be in some kind of trouble?" Frank asked.

"Not really," Rocco said. "We talked about how this school compared to Amberlin, which is much smaller, and then he left. He did seem a bit on edge, though, not his usual cheerful self. I asked him about his mood, but he said it was just the stress of being a stranger in a new place and not to worry about him."

"Do you know anything about his family?" Joe asked. "Maybe his parents have the kind of money that might attract kidnappers?"

Professor Rocco brushed at his mustache while he considered the question. "I really don't know. Eli is a very independent young man. He never talked about his family. Why, has there been a ransom demand from the kidnappers?"

Frank shook his head. "No, not yet anyway."

Frank and Joe asked a few more questions,

but the professor didn't seem to have any insight into Eli's disappearance.

"Well, thanks for your time, Professor," Frank said. "You might want to call the police and let them know about your connection with Eli."

"Good idea," Rocco said. "I'll do that. Thank you, boys, for letting me know about the situation. And please be in touch with any new developments."

"We sure will," Joe said with a wave as they left. "Thanks again. Goodbye."

On the way down the geology building stairs, Joe asked, "So, was that worth moving all those boxes?"

"I guess not," Frank said. "But at least we got a good workout."

"I'd rather do my weight lifting at the gym, where I can shower afterward," Joe said. "Why don't we head over to the incinerator site and try to find those two thugs from the S.A.C. office?"

"Good idea," Frank said.

They went back to the dorm to pick up their van. Richie was back, so he joined them for the trip.

Jessica's directions were easy to follow, but it took them forty-five minutes to make the twenty-mile trip because most of it was on back roads.

As the two-lane road turned into a dangerous S-curve that hugged the hillside to the left and edged along a ravine to the right, Frank said, "Can you imagine a semitrailer filled with leaky old rockets with nerve gas in them being driven on this road?"

Joe shook his head. "Talk about an accident waiting to happen. But if they built the incinerator close to a major highway and there was an accident, a lot more people could get hurt."

"True," Frank admitted. "I just think the whole idea is a mistake. There's got to be some way of getting rid of that nerve gas without burning it."

"I'm with you guys," Richie said. "Looks like they are, too." He pointed ahead to where a gravel access road led off the main road. They took the turnoff, and ahead of them they saw a twelve-foot-high chain-link fence with closed gates and security guards on the inside.

At least a hundred protesters of all ages had gathered outside the fence. Some marched and carried placards in front of the gates while others sat on blankets and lawn chairs, blocking the entrance.

"Not a bad-size group," Joe said as they pulled closer. "But a lot of them don't look like college students."

"They're probably local people who don't

want a nerve gas bonfire in their backyard,"
Richie said.

They pulled off the access road into an area
where dozens of other cars were parked in
rows among the weeds.

"Frank, look at that," Joe said. He pointed
to a beat-up green van parked halfway down
the row of cars in front of them.

Frank's jaw dropped. "That's the van the
kidnapper was driving," he said.

"It sure is," Joe said, jumping out of their
van.

Frank scrambled after his brother, with
Richie bringing up the rear. They jogged over
to the old green van and looked inside.

"Just like it was yesterday," Frank said,
spotting the spare tire where Eli had sat handcuffed. He went around to the side and saw
the ugly scrape where the van had smacked
into the parked sedan.

Joe found the driver's door unlocked. He
climbed in and looked around.

"The key's in the ignition," Joe said. "Other
than that, there's nothing but junk in here."
Then he sat on the passenger seat and popped
open the glove compartment, being careful to
push the button with his knuckle so as not to
leave a fingerprint. "Owner's manual and a few
spare fuses. Nothing to say who this rust
bucket belongs to."

41

Frank stood outside the passenger door considering their options. "We have to find out who owns it," he said. "One of us should keep watch here while the other two ask around."

Richie tapped him on the shoulder and pointed in the direction of the demonstration. "Why don't you just ask those guys?"

A dozen protesters were jogging toward the van, led by big Dale Shapley, who was wearing green camouflage fatigues covered with felt-pen graffiti, and his ponytailed crony, J. J. Nye. They heard Nye say, "Let's get them."

Joe jumped out of the green van, held up his hands, and said, "Hey, we were just—"

"You!" Shapley screamed, breaking into a run. "You better get away from my van or I'm going to rip your head off."

Chapter

5

FRANK STEPPED AWAY from the van, giving himself room to maneuver. Joe stood next to his brother while Richie took a seat on the trunk of a nearby car.

"I don't want to hurt anybody," Frank said quietly to Joe. "What do you say we try to avoid a fight?"

"I'm with you," Joe said, "but I don't think they're going to give us a choice."

Shapley stopped a couple of yards away from the Hardys, a cold smile on his doughy face. Nye hung back a step, and the others formed a loose semicircle behind them. Frank noticed another, larger group of protesters rushing over to join them.

A pale girl smoking a cigarette gestured excitedly at Frank and Joe. "Go ahead, Dale," she said. "Ask them why they were messing with your van."

"Forget it," Shapley said. Then he spat at Frank's feet. "You guys got off earlier today," he said, "but I'm ready for you this time."

"Why?" Joe said. "Did you skip lunch and get a brain transplant?"

Frank glanced sideways at Joe. He wanted him to keep that kind of wisecrack to himself, but he didn't have a chance to say anything because Shapley charged him right then, grabbed his shirt with both hands, and tried to lift him off his feet.

Frank brought both hands up inside Shapley's arms and chopped them down. At the same time he stuck one foot behind Shapley's leg, cut the big man's feet out from under him, and shoved hard.

Shapley toppled backward and rolled. Frank was on top of him before he could get up, grabbing his right wrist with both hands and twisting his arm up behind him. Shapley grunted in pain as Frank yanked up on his arm.

"Give up, Shapley," Frank said. "Don't make me break it."

"Get off me, punk," Shapley said through clenched teeth as he tried to wriggle out.

"I'm serious," Frank said. "I'll break your arm if I have to."

Nye stepped over to help Shapley, but Joe cut him off. The ponytailed thug narrowed his eyes and reached into his denim jacket. He pulled out a pair of foot-long black wooden rods joined by a short piece of chain—nunchakus.

"Out of my way," Nye snarled, "or I'll knock your teeth out." He snapped the chains in front of him.

Joe had seen that kind of weapon before and knew it could be dangerous. He stayed focused, though, and with a quick stab of his hand grabbed one of the rods. Then he jerked the other rod out of Nye's hand and spun the weapon off into the woods, way behind the rows of parked cars.

"Sorry," Joe said, "but I can't afford a trip to the dentist this week."

Stunned by Joe's quickness, Nye just stood and glared for a few seconds. Then his eyes darted around nervously.

Frank was still bent down, leaning into Shapley's bulk. He tightened his grip on Shapley's wrist and gave the arm another tug.

"All right," Shapley said, grimacing. "What do you want?"

"Just a few answers to a few questions," Frank said. "Why don't you start by telling us where you were around four o'clock yesterday afternoon?"

"None of your business," Shapley spat out, his jaw clenched against Frank's pressure on his arm.

"Try again," Joe said. "Your van was used in a kidnapping yesterday. We saw the whole thing. The driver was wearing a mask. He obviously wasn't a size extra large like you, Shapley. But it could easily have been Nye."

He looked confused. "That's crazy," he said. "I didn't kidnap anyone."

Joe shrugged and smiled. "Hey, you're probably telling the truth because you obviously don't have the guts *or* the brains to kidnap anyone. So why don't you humor me and tell me where you were at four o'clock yesterday?"

A few of the spectators snickered, and Nye's face started to turn red. He took two deep breaths, reared back, and threw a haymaker at Joe's jaw. Joe ducked, and Nye swung his other hand. This time Joe threw up his forearm and neatly blocked the punch. Nye threw a third roundhouse, and Joe slapped that one off to the side. Then Nye dropped back, breathing hard.

Joe straightened up, still smiling, and shot a solid right at Nye's nose, stopping it half an inch short. Nye stared cross-eyed at the rock-steady fist pointed just beyond the tip of his nose.

"We were hanging out at Dizzy Liz's coffeehouse," he said, "helping paint signs for today."

The girl with the cigarette said, "They weren't much help, but they were there all afternoon."

Several voices from the crowd backed them up: "I saw them." "They were there."

"So where was your van?" Frank asked Shapley.

"It was parked at our house," he said. "We walked to Dizzy Liz's."

"Who would have had access to it?" Frank asked, relaxing his grip on Shapley's arm.

"Anybody who wanted it," Shapley said. "I leave the key in it so I won't lose it. Who would be stupid enough to steal that thing anyway? We didn't get home until late last night, and it was there when we got back."

"Didn't you notice the scrape along the side?" Frank asked.

"Of course I did," Shapley said. "I saw it this morning, but I don't know how it got there."

"You were talking to Eli Travers on the mall a few hours before he was kidnapped," Joe said. "What did you talk about?"

Shapley didn't recognize the name, but after Joe described him he remembered the face.

"He was talking to the people in the S.A.C. booth," Shapley said. "We just told him that if he wanted to get anything done, he should hang around with us instead of those S.A.C. wimps."

Someone from the crowd called, "We're not the ones down on our knees in the mud," which got a few laughs.

Suddenly Nye looked earnest. "Hey, you know who you should talk to?" he said. "That girl . . . Jessica."

"We know," Joe said. "She talked to Eli in the booth."

"No, man," Nye said. "I mean, yeah, right. We were talking to him away from the booth. Then afterward she stopped him and started talking to him again, and they got into some kind of argument."

"J.J.'s right," Shapley said. "They had a fight. I bet she didn't tell you about *that.*"

Frank and Joe exchanged a look. They didn't want to admit it, but Shapley was right—Jessica hadn't told them about any argument. Frank loosened his grip on Shapley's wrist and let him up.

"All right, that's it from us," Frank said. "But you had better believe the cops are going

48

to be all over you after we tell them the kidnapping van belongs to you."

"Looks like they've got a pretty good alibi," Joe said. The Hardys were back in their van, headed for town. "Their friends in the crowd could have been lying to cover for them, though."

"True," Frank said, "but I think you were right, Joe. Shapley's too big to be the kidnapper, and Nye's too dumb and too scared."

"So that leaves us with zero suspects," Richie said.

"I'm interested in what they said about Jessica," Frank said.

Joe dismissed that with a wave. "Nye and Shapley got in a lot of trouble because of her. They hate her. They'd say anything to get even with her."

"I'll buy that," Frank said, "but it could work both ways. She's the one who sicced us on them. Besides, their story was too convincing to have been made up on the spot—especially by those two idiots."

"It probably is true," Joe said. "But so what? She saw Eli talking to those two and came out of the booth to warn him."

"So what was the argument about?" Frank said. "And why didn't she tell us about it?"

"Good question," Joe said. "Maybe we should try to find out."

"Our first stop is the police station," Frank said, "so we can let Mike DeFinis know we found the van and see if their investigation turned up anything new."

"Maybe they've been contacted by the kidnappers by now," Joe said.

They were only a few miles from Langston University, stopped at a traffic light just before the ramp to the interstate highway, when a limousine surrounded by a phalanx of police cars, lights flashing and sirens blaring, zoomed past.

"That's a major VIP," Joe said. "Probably General Albright."

"Good guess," Frank said. "Looks like they were coming from the airport."

"So what's the big deal with him anyway?" Joe asked.

Richie piped up from the backseat. "If you looked at the rest of the newspaper after the comics, you'd know."

"Hey," Joe said, "I read the sports section."

"Albright's been in the news a lot lately because of his work in Gabiz," Richie said as they pulled onto the highway.

"That's that African country where they're having a civil war," Joe said.

"Amazing," Richie said. "Where'd you read that? The funnies or the sports page?"

"Sports page," Joe said. "Central State recruited a top basketball player from Gabiz."

"Anyway," Frank said, "after years of war, both sides in Gabiz have agreed to a cease-fire, which Albright organized. He's supposed to go back to Gabiz next month, and everyone's pretty sure they'll sign a permanent peace agreement then."

"Don't forget he's also a graduate of Langston," Richie said. "He's going to give a speech on campus and be guest of honor at a fancy reception at the university president's house."

Frank grew quiet. He was concentrating on his driving, and Joe noticed him checking the rearview mirror a couple of times. At the next exit, he waited until the last possible second, then swerved into the far right lane and took the exit ramp.

"Hey, Frank," Richie said. "This isn't our exit."

Joe recognized the maneuver and, glancing out the back of the van, said, "Someone is tailing us."

Frank checked the rearview mirror again. "It's that two-tone sedan. He cut right in front of a semi to make that exit ramp."

"I can't see the driver," Joe said. There was too much glare off the other car's windshield.

51

"Let's take a closer look," Frank said.

At the next intersection, Frank took a right just as the light was changing. Then he pulled around the corner and stopped. Screened by a tall hedge that surrounded the house on the corner, he and Joe slipped out of the van.

"Drive around the block and pick us up," he said to Richie, who slid behind the wheel.

Frank and Joe slipped through the hedge and across the yard. Around the corner they saw the two-tone sedan waiting for the light to change. Joe crouched and ran around to the driver's side while Frank came up on the near side.

Before the startled driver could react, Joe reached through the open window, turned off the ignition, and plucked out the keys. The man behind the wheel, Joe suddenly realized, was the same guy they had chased through the parking garage that morning.

"All right," Joe said. "You owe us a few answers."

"I don't think so," the man said, his surprised expression turning ugly. He threw open the car door, knocking Joe back.

"I don't owe you a thing," the man snarled.

He pulled a black cylinder out of his pocket and stuck it in Joe's face.

"Get back, Joe," Frank shouted.

Chapter
6

JOE RECOGNIZED THE WEAPON right away. It was pepper spray, and if it caught him in the face it would turn him into a defenseless mess—or worse. He backed away, but the man kept coming, holding the shiny little canister at arm's length inches from Joe's nose.

Joe tripped and fell backward over the curb. He landed on his back in the street and propped himself up on his elbows. The man leaned over him and held the spray close to his face. "Give me the keys," he said. "Now."

Seeing his brother was about to be blinded by chemical spray, Frank vaulted onto the hood of the car, took one giant stride, and launched himself at Joe's assailant. The man must have weighed over two hundred pounds, but Frank hit him hard and they went down in a tangle.

Two loud blasts from a car horn brought Frank scrambling to his feet. Joe's attacker stood up, too, and started looking around frantically. Frank realized he must have dropped his chemical spray.

"Are you looking for this?" Joe asked. He was leaning against the hood of the car, holding the canister in his right hand. The man cast a surly glance at Joe and said, "Just give me my keys."

"Sorry, not until you tell us why you've been following us," Joe said.

"Have it your way," the man said. He went to the driver's-side door, reached in the open window, and pulled out a car phone. "You're under investigation for acts of vandalism committed at the Four Winds incinerator site. I was holding off bringing the police into this, but you're not giving me any choice."

The Hardys looked at each other and smiled. "So go ahead and call the cops," Joe said. "You might save yourself some time by asking for Detective Loomis or Officer DeFinis."

The man held the phone to his ear and watched them with narrowed eyes.

Frank pulled out his wallet and held up his ID for the man to see. "I'm Frank Hardy, and this is my brother, Joe. We're involved in an investigation, too. We're willing to work with you if you'll work with us."

The Hardys' sudden cooperation seemed to make the man even more suspicious. When he got through to the police station, however, he did ask for Detective Loomis or Officer DeFinis. There was a brief pause.

"Officer DeFinis," he said into the phone, "this is Amos Thorpe. I'm a private investigator working for Julian Construction, the builders of the Four Winds incinerator facility. I'm investigating acts of vandalism at the site, and I'm with two suspects. They identified themselves as Frank and Joe Hardy."

Frank and Joe managed to stifle their impatience as Thorpe listened. He shook his head and uttered an occasional "I see." Finally, he said, "Thanks, Officer."

"Mind if I speak to him?" Frank said as Thorpe was about to hang up. Thorpe handed Frank the phone.

"Hi, Mike," Frank said. "We made a positive ID on the owners of that green van used in the Eli Travers kidnapping. They're J. J. Nye and Dale Shapley. They used to be Langston students. They still have some connection with the Student Action Committee there. And at least one of them—Shapley—has a police record."

"Thanks, Frank," DeFinis said. "We'll look into it. You guys take care now."

"Mike, is there anything new on the kidnapping?"

"Not that I know of."

"Okay, thanks. We'll be in touch."

" 'Bye now."

" 'Bye." Frank handed the phone back to Thorpe, who hung it up inside his car. Then Joe gave Thorpe his car keys and chemical spray.

"Well," Thorpe said, clearing his throat as Richie pulled up to the curb in the Hardys' van. "I'm glad we got our little misunderstanding all worked out. Would you fellows like to join me for something to eat? It's on me."

"Sure," Joe said.

"Why not?" Frank said.

They introduced Thorpe to Richie. Then they all headed to a nearby diner.

"I was checking out the S.A.C. offices on campus," Thorpe told them over their slices of pecan pie. "They've been organizing most of the protests at the site, so I figured that was the first place to look for suspects. I got there this morning and saw you three go in. Two other guys came out, and I decided to have a chat with them."

56

"Nye and Shapley," Frank said.

"Those aren't the names they gave me," Thorpe said, "but I never had a chance to check their IDs. I asked them about the S.A.C. and the problems at the site. They told me a couple of guys from a militant environmental group were on campus to work with the head of the Student Action Committee. They described you two, said you were ecoterrorists. So when you came out, I tailed you."

"Maybe those two aren't so stupid after all," Frank said to Joe. "We had a little run-in with them in the S.A.C. office this morning," he explained to Thorpe. "So when they met you, they figured that was their perfect chance to set us up."

Joe pushed his empty dish away. "So you're a private eye," he said to Thorpe. "What was with that James Bond escape from the parking garage? Somebody could have been hurt."

Thorpe nodded. "I admit I got a little carried away," he said. "But what did I know? Those guys had just told me you two were expert saboteurs. Then you started chasing me. I didn't want you to blow my cover."

Frank sipped his soda and then asked, "So, has there been any real sabotage going on at the site?"

Thorpe scratched his head. "Well, this isn't common knowledge, but from what Officer

DeFinis said, you guys are in the clear and you might be able to help. Just keep it quiet, all right?"

"You have our word," Joe said.

"It started out as a few random acts—two hydraulic hoses cut on equipment, a couple of windows broken on the construction trailer, air let out of some tires. Then one day the engines started locking up on all of the heavy machinery. Someone had filled the oil filters with sand. That cost a lot of time and money to fix. They beefed up security at the site. Then, earlier this week, they were moving bundles of steel structural supports with a crane when the chains holding the bundles snapped. It turned out someone had used a hacksaw to weaken the chains on several bundles. They're lucky nobody got seriously hurt. That's when I was called in."

"We had another run-in with Nye and Shapley out at the site earlier," Frank said. "They're suspects in a possible kidnapping of a student."

"I think you might want to follow *them* around for a while," Joe said.

"I think you're right," Thorpe said. "Thanks for the tip."

The Hardys and Richie thanked Thorpe for the pie and went back to the dorm. They tried to reach Officer DeFinis to follow up on their tip about Shapley's van. He was out, but they left a message, and he returned their call an hour later.

"Loomis and the feds brought Nye and Shapley in for questioning," DeFinis told Frank over the phone. "They had to cut them loose, though. Lots of people saw them at Dizzy Liz's, so it looks like their alibi is good."

"Has anybody turned up any other suspects?" Frank asked.

"Not that I know of," DeFinis said. "They managed to contact Eli's father. He was out of the country on business, and he's flying back now. It turns out he's a pretty powerful businessman, on the boards of directors of a number of companies. Loomis is pretty sure the kidnappers are in it for the money, so he's waiting for a ransom note."

"Thanks again, Mike," Frank said. "We'll talk to you soon. 'Bye."

Richie decided they could all use some exercise, so he took the Hardys to the basketball courts behind the dorm, where they shot around and discussed the case.

As soon as they hit the court, Joe grabbed the ball from Richie and drove hard for the far basket. Frank chased Joe the length of the court and reached in to poke the ball away. But Joe pulled up inside the foul line and buried a soft jumper.

"I don't care about the alibi," Joe said as they took turns shooting twenty-footers. "It has to be Nye and Shapley. Maybe the people at Dizzy Liz's lied to the police, or maybe Nye sneaked out long enough to kidnap Eli, then got back before anyone missed him."

Richie went high to grab a rebound and passed it out to Frank, who backed in on Joe.

"I don't think it was them," Frank said over his shoulder. "I think it was them," Frank said over his shoulder. "I think someone wants us to *think* it's them. Why would Nye and Shapley use their van, which everybody knows, for a kidnapping right on campus in broad daylight?"

He faked right, spun left, and slipped past Joe for an easy layup.

"Besides," Frank added, "why would they want to kidnap Eli in the first place?"

Richie tried for a three-pointer that bounced off the heel of the rim. Joe went up quickly and grabbed the rebound.

"Ransom," Joe said, dribbling the ball warily as he approached Frank and Richie. "Or maybe he met with them after he talked to them on the mall and he saw something or heard something he wasn't supposed to, maybe something that connects them to the sabotage at the construction site. Or maybe they let him in on the secret and asked him to join them.

He turned them down, and they had to get him out of the way so he wouldn't tell anyone."

Joe drove the lane and went up for a shot, but Frank got his hands up and caught a piece of the ball, which flew into Richie's hands.

"I'm not disagreeing with you, Joe," Frank said. "But I think there's more to this, and we should keep an open mind."

Joe wiped the sweat out of his eyes and stood a few feet from his brother. "Open to what?"

Frank shrugged. "Don't forget the argument with Eli that Jessica didn't mention to us. What if she's involved somehow? We know Nye and Shapley hate her, and it's a pretty good bet she hates them, too."

"Right," Richie said. "What if she framed them? She probably knows about the van. If she found out Nye and Shapley were at Dizzy Liz's, she could have borrowed the van, worn the mask—"

"And shot at Frank so he had to jump off the back of the van at forty miles an hour and almost get himself killed?" Joe said. "You've got to be kidding."

"Maybe she hired somebody who went a little too far," Richie said. "Just as Amos Thorpe went a little too far with the umbrella chase."

"All right," Joe said. "If Jessica and whoever she hired kidnapped Eli, then where are they hiding him?"

"I'm not saying I think she kidnapped Eli," Richie replied. "I'm just saying I agree with Frank, that we don't know everything that's going on and that Jessica is probably involved somehow. Okay, your Nye-and-Shapley motive is better than the one I came up with for Jessica. But their alibi checks out. Jessica's the one who's hiding something."

"That's right, Joe" Frank said. "I say we hurry up and find out what she's hiding and why."

"All right," Joe said. "How about tomorrow you go ask Jessica about her argument with Eli? Me, I'll follow Nye and Shapley and see if they lead me to him."

"Sounds good," Frank said. "Now, are we going to play some hoops or not?"

Joe was ready to get back in the game, but Richie was sitting on the ball now, his elbows resting on his knees.

"Come on, Richie," Joe said. "How about a little game of twenty-one before dinner?"

They shot for another half hour and then went back to the dorm to eat. After dinner they spent the rest of the evening relaxing in Richie's room, quizzing him about campus life, then reading and watching some TV.

They turned in just before midnight, Richie

in his bed and the Hardys in their sleeping bags on the floor. Joe was thinking about the next day, trying to plan his surveillance of Nye and Shapley. It had been a long day, though, and he fell asleep within a couple of minutes.

Hours later Joe woke up, disoriented. The first thing he noticed was that it was too warm in his sleeping bag. He knew it wasn't anywhere near morning yet. His throat felt dry, and he thought he heard crackling and hissing sounds behind him.

Suddenly he sat up and turned around.

When he did, a wave of heat slapped him in the face and he saw flames shooting out from the curtains at one end of the room.

Chapter

7

"FRANK, RICHIE! Wake up!" Joe shouted hoarsely as he struggled out of his sleeping bag. "The room's on fire."

The flames were eating up the curtains and licking the ceiling. Thick black smoke was everywhere.

Joe pushed himself to his knees, got a mouthful of smoke, and started to cough.

"Just stay low," came Frank's voice. Joe could make out the figure of his brother crawling toward Richie's head.

Joe found the door and groped for the dead-bolt knob. He couldn't turn it. He leaned down and inhaled a breath of fresh air from underneath the door. Then he stood up and put all of his strength into turning the knob.

It wouldn't budge. He dropped back down to his hands and knees. The curtains were a solid wall of flame now, and the fire was spreading over the walls and across the ceiling.

Joe's eyes were watering, his head felt light, and the heat was pressing down on him like a deadly weight. He could see Frank and Richie crawling across the floor on their bellies.

"The bolt's jammed," Joe said. "I can't force it open."

"Let me try," Frank said.

Joe moved aside. He knew if he couldn't turn it, Frank wouldn't be able to, either. But he let Frank go ahead and try while he crawled back to his sleeping bag.

Shielding his face from the heat, he dug through his knapsack until he found his pocketknife.

Frank and Richie were staying low and pounding on the door with their fists.

Joe crawled over, took a few more breaths from underneath the door, and flipped open the sturdiest blade on his knife. He used the blade to work the pin out of the door's bottom hinge. Then he gulped another breath of fresh air, stood up, and wriggled the pin free on the upper hinge. His lungs bursting, Joe yanked the door open.

A rain of pennies jingled to the floor, and a huge cloud of smoke billowed out of the room.

Frank and Richie stumbled out into the hallway. Joe followed, staggering and collapsing against a wall. He was dimly aware of doors opening up and down the hallway, people shouting, and the resident assistant running half-dressed into Richie's room with a fire extinguisher. As Joe struggled to catch his breath, he couldn't get one question out of his mind: Where had all those pennies come from?

He got his answer half an hour later, after the fire department had come and finished putting out the blaze. Joe, Frank, and Richie lay on cots set up in a friend's room while Detective Loomis questioned them about the fire. Joe mentioned the pennies.

"It's a dorm prank," Richie explained. "See, if someone has the dead bolt locked on his door, you push on the door at the top and the bottom as hard as you can, and you fill the space between the door and the frame with pennies. It puts so much force on the dead bolt that you can't turn the knob, and whoever's inside is trapped."

"How about setting the curtains on fire?" Joe asked. "Is that part of the prank?"

"I think that's a new twist," Richie said.

"Any idea how the fire started?" Frank asked the detective.

Loomis referred to his notebook. "According to the firefighters, some sort of accelerant was sprayed through the screen of the open window and then ignited."

"But that's a third-floor window," Joe said.

The detective nodded. "There wasn't any evidence of someone climbing up or using a ladder. The arsonist probably lowered himself down from the roof. It's only one floor up."

The detective finished taking their statements. "You boys stay out of trouble and be sure to call me if anything else comes up," he said as he got up to leave.

After Loomis left, Joe turned to Frank and said, "I'd say somebody just came pretty close to burning the three of us alive. Do you think they'd go that far just to keep us from snooping around about Eli?"

"Why else would anyone go after us?" Frank asked. "They must think we're getting close to uncovering something."

Joe lay down on his cot and stared up at the ceiling. "Now we just have to figure out what it is."

"And who would think that," Frank added.

The next morning Richie went to file a report about his room with dorm management. Frank and Joe split up as planned. Frank called the S.A.C. office and got Jessica's home phone number. He gave her a call and told her he needed to talk to her in person. She told him to come right over and gave him directions.

Jessica's house was a five-minute walk from campus. As Frank turned the corner onto her street, he saw two men in dark suits and dark glasses, wearing tiny earphones—just like Secret Service agents. Frank saw two more security men in the same dark suits farther down the block. He couldn't be sure because of the sunglasses, but he had a definite feeling they were all watching him.

Several sedans with tinted windows were parked at the curb in front of a small house a few doors down the street. Two more security men stood guard on the lawn, one on either side of the front porch.

Frank stopped in front of the guarded house and checked Jessica's address, which he had written on a small piece of paper. This was the place. With all these agents, he wondered if something was wrong.

He approached one of the security men stationed by the porch and said, "Hi. My name's Frank Hardy. Jessica is expecting me."

Without looking at him, the man held up his hand and said something about a guest arrival into a small transmitter pinned under his jacket lapel. He pressed one finger to his earphone, listened for a moment, then said, "Okay, Mr. Hardy. Please enter the house and wait in the living room. Ms. Albright will be with you shortly."

Suddenly it all made sense. Jessica's name was Albright—as in General Sean Albright.

"Thank you, sir," Frank said as he stepped up to the porch and let himself into the house. The living room was comfortably furnished but not fancy. It was exactly what Frank would have expected for two fairly well-to-do college students. Frank took a seat on the faded sofa and glanced at the array of mail, magazines, and notes covering the long wooden crate that served as a coffee table.

A girl with long brown hair and curls stepped into the living room.

"Oh," she said, pausing when she saw Frank sitting on the sofa. "You must be Frank. I'm Pam, Jessica's roommate."

A flurry of angry shouting came from the back of the house. Frank could pick out two voices—a booming male one that was answered by a strong female one.

"Jessica and her father are bonding at the moment," Pam said with a slight smile. "She should be out in a few minutes."

"Thanks," Frank said. "I take it the two of them don't get along very well."

"That's one way of putting it." Pam sat cross-legged on the big overstuffed chair across from Frank. "He has big political plans for her and thinks she's screwing them up by making herself look like a troublemaker."

"So they argue a lot?"

"Only when they're together," Pam said. "Oh, they love each other and all that, but pick pretty much any issue, and they'll probably be on opposite sides of it. She thinks he's too controlling, and he thinks she's too rebellious. They're both stubborn. It makes for some interesting family reunions."

The sound of a door opening down the hallway drew their attention in that direction. Sharp, measured footsteps sounded on the wooden floor, and then General Albright appeared.

Frank had seen the general's picture in newspapers and magazines. He was a handsome man with a strong chin. His dark hair was streaked with gray, cut short, and combed straight back. He was wearing a navy blue suit and a red tie.

What the pictures didn't show was his commanding presence. He was a trim man of average height and build, but like a much bigger man, he completely dominated the space around him. He was obviously used to being in charge.

"Who are you?" the general snapped, his stony gray eyes fixed on Frank.

"I'm Frank Hardy," he said, rising. "I'm here to see Jess—"

"Fine," the general said. Then he grumbled something and, with a backhand wave, turned and walked out of the house.

As Frank stood blinking, Jessica appeared from the hallway. Pam excused herself.

"Sorry, Frank," Jessica said. "Dad can be a little gruff sometimes."

"I got that impression," Frank said with a smile and a shake of his head.

"He's just upset about our protest against the incinerator," she said. "He thinks it looks bad for me to speak out against something he supports so strongly. Like the rest of the military, he thinks there's not much risk in the waste-disposal program. He's giving a speech tonight at the arena to make a case for the incinerator. We're going to be there to protest. Unfortunately, Dad can be very convincing."

"To most people but not to you," Frank said.

Jessica gave a halfhearted laugh. "True. I guess I'm immune. So why did you want to see me? Have you learned anything new about your friend Eli?"

Frank shook his head; Jessica seemed disappointed.

"We took your advice and went looking for Nye and Shapley at the incinerator site yesterday," Frank said. "We had another run-in with them. It got kind of physical."

71

"You mean you guys got into a fight with them?" she said.

"Well, not exactly," Frank said. "Let's just say they were looking to mix it up and we sort of talked them out of it." He paused.

"Jessica," Frank continued, "Nye and Shapley said you had an argument with Eli before he was kidnapped. Mind if I ask what that was all about?"

"It wasn't anything," she said, glancing away. "I saw Eli talking to those two jerks and tried to warn him about them. But he seemed to be buying their macho baloney, so I got a little frustrated and a little upset. That's all."

"How long did you say you've known Eli?"

She looked puzzled. "I told you, I just met him that morning," she said. "I never saw him before then."

Frank nodded. "Would you mind telling me everything you know about Eli? Any little detail could help."

"Look," she said, backing toward the hallway. "I've already told you everything I know. I only talked to him for a few minutes. Now, if that's all you want, I'll have to excuse myself and get back to work. I've got to get organized for the protest at the arena tonight."

She turned and left without waiting for Frank to respond. Just as well, Frank decided. What else could he say? Her story was reasonable enough, but he still felt there was more to it. Maybe she was just busy with the protest and distracted because of the argument with her father. Or maybe she really was holding something back.

As he went out the door and down the porch steps, Frank wondered if Joe was having better luck than he was.

Joe had started his day early, staking out Nye and Shapley's house. Within the first half hour the pair had hopped into their van and left.

At first Joe, following in his own van, thought they were on their way to the incinerator site, but they ended up following back roads a little over ten miles from the Langston campus to a small abandoned airfield, its single runway overgrown with weeds. Nye and Shapley parked behind a dingy gray Quonset hut, where they were out of sight of the gravel access road. Joe drove past, parked in the woods, and sneaked back through the underbrush to get a closer look at the hut.

He saw Nye and Shapley's van parked by the hut but no sight of them. He darted from the woods to the side of the hut and edged up close to one of the windows.

He had to press his face almost up against the grimy glass and shield his eyes with his hands to make out anything inside. The interior was lit by some kind of camp lantern. Shapley was standing at a long table or workbench with his back to the window. Joe peered at the table but couldn't make out what he was working on.

Frustrated, Joe decided to try another window. As he straightened and backed up a step, though, he felt a pair of powerful arms lock around his neck and shoulders, pulling him off balance. He tried to shake himself free, but the grip just got tighter.

He wanted to turn and get a look at his attacker, but suddenly two fingers dug into the side of his neck. He felt the pulse pounding in his artery. This guy was good, Joe remembered thinking as the pressure mounted, cutting off circulation to his brain. In an instant Joe's vision went blurry, and then everything went black.

Joe woke up to a violent bouncing sensation. His head felt fuzzy, and he was disoriented. He looked around him and realized he was back in his own van. How had he gotten there?

Struggling to focus, he looked straight ahead, out the windshield. He realized the van was hurtling down a grassy hillside, bouncing off rocks and gullies. It was headed straight for the churning brown waters of a river, and one of Joe's wrists was handcuffed to the steering wheel.

Chapter

8

JOE GRABBED the steering wheel with both hands, but it was locked. Then he stomped hard on the brake pedal. He guessed the van was going at least thirty miles an hour, and with the power off, he would have to apply a lot of pressure to make the brakes respond.

Joe planted both feet on the pedal and slammed on the brakes as hard as he could. The van slowed, but it didn't stop. Another twenty-five yards and he would plunge into the river.

He smashed the emergency brake to the floor with his left foot and heard a grinding screech of metal on metal. Less than ten yards to go and the van was still rolling.

Joe's palms were so sweaty that he lost his grip on the steering wheel and had to brace his free hand against the roof in order to jam both feet down on the brake pedal again. The van finally shuddered to a halt.

Joe couldn't see the edge of the riverbank—all he could see was water. He slammed the gearshift into park, closed his eyes, took a deep breath, and sat back in his seat. Then he reached for the car phone to call for help.

Within half an hour Joe was leaning against a county police car. The tow-truck operator had cut the handcuffs off, and now the men were winching the van back up to the road. Frank and Richie had shown up, thanks to a ride from Officer Mike DeFinis.

"Our insurance company is going to love this one," Joe said.

"What happened?" Frank asked. "We were in Richie's old room, going through the mess when Mike called us. He said he heard on the police band that you almost drove the van into the river and that you were trapped or something."

Joe told him about following Nye and Shapley to the Quonset hut and how he was attacked from behind with a choke hold.

"It must have been Nye," Richie said.

"I don't think so," Frank said. "That kind

76

of choke hold is tricky. The attacker had to be an expert martial artist. If you hold it just a few seconds too long, it can easily kill."

Joe rubbed his neck with a grimace. "Nye is no expert. It had to be somebody else."

"Come on," DeFinis said. "Let's go check out this Quonset hut."

They all piled into the police cruiser, Joe sitting up front. DeFinis pulled out a map, and Joe showed him where the Quonset hut was.

"Any new developments on the kidnapping?" Frank asked once they were under way.

"Yep," DeFinis said. "Eli's father arrived in town yesterday."

"Has there been a ransom demand?" Joe asked.

"Still nothing," DeFinis said. "That's what's making Detective Loomis suspicious. That, and his talk with Eli's father. Mr. Travers was not at all surprised to hear about his son's involvement with the Student Action Committee. At his last college Eli got into a lot of trouble supporting all kinds of causes."

"Like what?" Frank said.

"He stopped the homecoming parade by organizing a human chain to block the street. He claimed the school was cutting aid to low-income students and using the money to build a new football stadium. Another time, he started a campus-wide boycott of products made by certain companies because he said those companies dealt with countries that were committing human-rights violations. And get this: his father is on the board of directors of two of those companies."

"That must make for interesting dinner-table conversation in the Travers household," Richie said.

"Sort of like the relationship between Jessica Albright and her father, the general," Frank said.

"Jessica *Albright?*" Joe said, turning to Richie in the backseat.

"Her father, the general?" Richie said, raising his eyebrows.

"You got that right, fellas," Frank said. "Jessica is the general's daughter, *and* she's organizing a demonstration tonight to protest his speech defending the incinerator project. That's all she'd tell me. That and that she doesn't know anything more about Eli. She said she was trying to warn him not to mess with Nye and Shapley, and that's why they got into an argument."

Frank turned back to DeFinis. "Were there any other developments?"

"There was a break-in at the university president's house last night," the officer said. "When he and his wife got home, they found the back door busted open. He called the police, and there was a search, but they didn't catch anybody."

"Was anything taken?" Joe asked.

"No, but the burglar used a credit card to try to jimmy open a glass case containing rare coins. The card snapped, and half of it fell into the case. It belonged to Eli Travers."

"So Eli goes from being a supposed kidnap victim to being a burglar," Richie said.

"Hold on," Frank said. "Anybody could have used that card."

"True," DeFinis said. "But after what his father said and because there's been no ransom demand and because of Eli's connection with Nye and Shapley, Detective Loomis is starting to think that he staged his own kidnapping."

Joe shook his head. "What would be the point of that?"

"I don't know," DeFinis said. "Loomis thinks maybe he was going to use the coins to pull some kind of Robin Hood stunt, give them to somebody he thought the university was taking money away from or something."

"That's baloney," Joe said. "We saw the look on his face when he was forced into the van. No way was he faking that."

"Did his father mention whether Eli has any martial arts training?" Frank said.

Richie gave him a strange look. "Now, hold on, Frank," he said. "Are you saying it was Eli who used the choke hold on Joe at the Quonset hut?"

Frank shrugged. "We pretty much decided that it wasn't Nye, and Shapley was in the hut at the time. There had to be somebody else out there. Anybody with martial arts training would be a good candidate."

They reached the Quonset hut within ten minutes. Nye and Shapley's van was gone. So was the lantern that Shapley had used, and there was so much dust and grime on the windows of the hut that DeFinis had to lead them inside with his flashlight.

"They cleaned the place out," Joe said as the flashlight beam played over the bare workbench. He borrowed the light for a closer look as the others wandered back out into the sunlight.

"Any idea who owns this place?" Frank asked DeFinis as they stood by the rusty corrugated steel door.

"I think the county does," the officer said, "but it hasn't been used in decades, since they opened the new airport over by the university."

Frank kicked the fluff off a dandelion and watched it drift away. "So there's no telling how long they might have been using this place or what for."

"Maybe not," Joe said as he emerged from the hut, "but these might help. I found them under the workbench." He held out his palm. In it were three snips of red wire less than an inch long.

"Good work, Joe," Frank said.

"Let's see," DeFinis said, holding out his hand. Joe handed him two of the snippets and carefully pocketed the other one before anyone noticed.

"It's not much, but it's better than nothing," the officer said. "Let's head back, guys. I'm going to have to file these in the evidence room."

Joe's wild ride down the hillside had broken a spring in the van and caused some other minor damage, but by dinner time it was ready for action again. So were the Hardys.

General Albright's speech was scheduled for eight o'clock at the Langston University basketball arena. Frank, Joe, and Richie were curious about what sort of protest Jessica and the S.A.C. were planning.

After a quick meal back at the dorm, they drove over to the arena and pulled into its parking lot. Not far away the S.A.C. had stationed a flatbed truck, which was draped with

81

banners showing the incinerator churning out lethal smoke and surrounded by barren countryside. Jessica Albright stood on the truck's bed, giving a speech through a megaphone. Referring to notes in her hand, she was listing all the possible dangers of the incinerator program.

"She sure is a lot more focused than she was this morning," Frank said as they threaded their way through the crowd that was gathering around the flatbed truck.

"No kidding," Joe said. "She's really getting this crowd warmed up. Her father's going to have a tough act to follow."

They headed into the arena and took three seats in the balcony. Rows of chairs had been set up on the basketball court and a stage erected at one end. The stage was empty, but the seats were almost full and there was a buzz in the air. At least fifty people—most of them appeared to be students—were milling up and down the aisles, some of them holding up banners and signs, others handing out leaflets.

A long, piercing blast from an air horn made everybody jump. Frank tried to determine where it had come from.

"Nye and Shapley," Joe said, pointing them out. "See them?" They were on the main floor, not far from the stage. Nye had just handed the horn to Shapley, who let out another blast. They were quickly surrounded by campus cops.

"There's another familiar face," Frank said. "Right down there."

Occupying a seat at the edge of the balcony several rows in front of them was Professor Rocco.

"Let's go say hi," Joe said.

Professor Rocco was leaning forward in his seat watching the activity on the main floor when they approached. He was a little startled when they greeted him but quickly regained his composure. Typical university professor, Joe thought: a little excitement and it throws him completely off his stride.

"Good evening," the professor said. "It's awfully busy around here tonight, isn't it?"

"I guess so," Joe said.

"It's a little overwhelming," Rocco said. "At Amberlin, I don't think there are as many people in the whole school as there are in this arena tonight."

"It must be pretty exciting for you," Frank said. "I was wondering—as a professor of environmental science, what do you think about the incinerator program?"

"I really haven't had an opportunity to study it in depth," he said, "so I can't comment authoritatively. Of course, there are two sides to every issue. It's not always the obvious position that's correct. It really pays to examine all the available data before one chooses sides." He paused to let those words sink in, then said, "How goes the search for Eli? Have you heard anything?"

"There hasn't been any word from the kidnappers," Frank said. "Some people think Eli might have staged his own abduction. There was a break-in at President Baker's house last night. They found part of a credit card there that belonged to Eli."

"How strange," Rocco said.

The general and his entourage emerged onto the main floor and took up their positions on the stage.

"I guess we'd better get back to our seats," Joe said. "Nice to see you again, Professor Rocco."

When they sat down, Frank and Joe saw two campus cops leading Nye and Shapley out of the arena.

"I guess our friends were *dis*invited for the speech," Joe said.

The rest of the protesters had been ushered to the sides and back of the arena, where they stood quietly, waving their signs and banners under the watchful eyes of the campus police.

University President Baker stood at the lectern and gave General Albright a flattering ten-minute introduction, reviewing all of his many accomplishments in war and diplomacy. It was followed by polite applause from most of the audience.

Then the general took the lectern. Far from the gruff, granite-faced man Frank had encountered that morning, he proved to be a warm and charismatic speaker. He spoke of the disposal of chemical weapons as a necessary step in the evolution of world peace. The incinerator program, he explained, represented an important contribution to this process from the local community. He made any and all supporters of the program out to be heroes of the peace process and downplayed any potential dangers of the program.

The general's speech went on for twenty-five minutes. After the applause died down, he held a ten-minute question-and-answer session, even fielding several tough questions from the protesters.

"That man sure can talk," Richie said, as he, Frank, and Joe walked out to the parking lot afterward. "Now there will probably be people protesting the protesters: 'I'm a patriotic American. Don't take away my incinerator.'"

Although Richie was joking, Frank thought he did have a point. The general's speech seemed to have calmed many of the fears of those in the audience. The crowd around the

S.A.C. truck was much smaller than when they had walked past it the first time, though Jessica still spoke with a passion that rivaled her father's charm.

They reached the van and had started to get in when a campus cop stepped up to Frank and said, "Did you get it fixed?"

"What?"

"Your van. Did you get it fixed? I thought I saw you working on it last time I walked by. I can radio for a tow truck if you need one."

"I'm sorry, Officer," Frank said, "but I have no idea what you're talking about."

"Just a few minutes ago," the officer explained, "I walked past here and saw a pair of legs sticking out from under this van. I was headed over to check out a car alarm that was going off. Otherwise I would have stopped to help."

"Hold on just a second," Frank said. "May I borrow your flashlight?"

"Sure," the officer said, handing it to him. "Are you saying that wasn't you under the van?"

"That's exactly what I'm saying," Frank said, his voice muffled as he slid under the van and shone the flashlight up under it. He shifted his position a couple of times, searching behind the exhaust pipe, axles, muffler, and gas tank.

"See anything, Frank?" Joe asked, bending

down and supporting himself with his hands on his knees.

Frank spotted two flashing red lights up beside where the rear axle connected to the chassis. It was the digital readout from a timer. A set of wires led from the timer to a small package attached to the gas tank.

"It's a bomb," Frank said, glancing back at the timer. "We've got less than thirty seconds until it blows."

Chapter

9

FRANK FIGURED there was enough plastic explosive in the package to splatter everything within a fifty-foot radius.

"I'm going to try to defuse this thing," Frank said.

"Want some help?" Joe said.

"Just clear the area as best you can," Frank said, pulling out his pocketknife.

Joe sprinted back to the S.A.C. truck, leaped up onto the bed, and snatched the megaphone away from a startled Jessica Albright.

"Your attention, please," Joe said into the megaphone. "Everybody please stay calm. There is a bomb in this parking lot. Please calmly walk back to the arena and go inside. I repeat: a bomb has been found under a car. Please turn around and go inside. Please walk quickly and calmly back to the arena."

Joe kept repeating the message until he was sure everyone within earshot had heard it. He could see the campus police doing their best to hustle everyone back inside the arena without causing mass panic.

Underneath the van Frank studied the wires linking the timer to the explosives, comparing this setup to some basic bomb-wiring schemes he'd studied. The counter reached the single digits as he traced each of the five thin intertwined wires that snaked out of the timer.

Unfortunately, the connection to the detonator was hidden behind the package of explosives. He knew he should check that first, but he was sure it had been set to detonate on contact. So instead of moving the package, he'd just have to make a good guess.

Frank knew there was one wire he didn't want to clip because it would short-circuit the detonator and blow the whole thing, but he didn't know which one it was. He decided to cut the blue one. It was his favorite color. He carefully separated it from the others and snipped it clean with two seconds left on the timer.

Frank stared as the digital readout flickered

down to zero. It stopped blinking, the timer let out three short beeps, and—nothing happened.

Frank let out a lungful of air, let his head fall back on the asphalt, and rested there for a couple of seconds. Once the tension had drained from his body, he slowly pulled himself out from under the van.

Joe was waiting right there next to it.

"I thought I told you to clear—" Frank said.

"Hey," Joe said. "I knew you weren't going to let the van blow up. Not after we just got it fixed this afternoon."

Within seconds they were surrounded by campus cops. Detective Loomis, along with several other town police officers, arrived a few minutes later.

The detective questioned the campus officer who had seen the pair of legs under the Hardys' van. But other than the fact that the person had been wearing blue jeans, he couldn't recall any details. He couldn't even be sure whether the person under the van had been a man or a woman. The detective went to confer with the other officers and with two security men in suits whom Frank recognized as members of General Albright's entourage.

An officer from the bomb squad was working under the van. He soon emerged with the disassembled device.

"Nice job," he said to Frank. "If you'd cut

any one of those other wires . . . *boom*—see you later."

"Tell me something," Joe said to the bomb expert. "Does this match any of the wires in the bomb?" He held out one of the snips of wire he had found at the Quonset hut that morning.

After a quick comparison, the officer said, "No, I'm afraid not."

"Did you find anything traceable under there?" Frank asked.

"Not that I can tell on first look," he said. "The FBI will be looking into that in more detail, though. From what I can see, your bomber knew what he was doing. These components are pretty common."

The Hardys thanked him and joined Richie, who was sitting on the back of a police car.

"What do you guys think?" Joe asked. "Nye and Shapley could have hung around the parking lot and planted the bomb. Jessica and a lot of the S.A.C. people were out here the whole time. One of them could have done it."

"Or seen who did it," Frank said. "Either way, this definitely proves we're up against somebody with professional skills. Whoever it is knows martial arts and knows how to make bombs."

"He also does a pretty good Spider-Man imitation," Richie said. "He climbed down—or up—to my window and set my room on fire."

"It could be more than one person," Frank said.

"It could be three or four people," Joe said.

"Whatever, they've got some impressive skills," Frank said.

"I wonder who these guys are and what they want," Richie said.

"We'd better hurry up and find out before somebody gets seriously hurt," Joe said. "Come on, let's get out of here."

Richie had been temporarily assigned to a new room while his was under repair. After spending the night in the new room, the Hardys went with Richie to help him finish sorting through the mess in his old room.

The whole window area was charred. The two dressers were as black as charcoal on the outside, but the contents hadn't burned. The cardboard boxes still holding most of Richie's and Eli's stuff were drenched from the fire hoses. Anything that wasn't singed by the fire or soaked by the water was saturated with smoke.

"Forget about our sleeping bags," Frank said. "They're a lost cause."

"Why am I not surprised?" Joe said. He was going through Eli's things, moving whatever was salvageable to fresh cardboard boxes. He had already emptied the dressers and was working on the desk, which was mostly untouched by the fire. He found a scrapbook in one of the drawers. It was filled with newspaper accounts of various protests Eli had been in.

"Hey, Frank," Joe said, "check this out."

He passed the scrapbook to Frank. It was open to an article about a demonstration in Washington, D.C., protesting U.S. military involvement in the civil war in Gabiz.

"Interesting," Frank said. "Does it mention the names of any of the protesters?"

"No," Joe said, "but a lot of the other articles in there do mention Eli by name. He must have been involved in the Gabiz protest. Otherwise, why would he have saved the article?"

"Maybe he was planning for the future," Frank said.

"Or checking out the competition," Joe said.

"Whatever," Frank said. He kept leafing through the scrapbook, and Joe went back to emptying Eli's desk. A few minutes later Joe pulled out an item that stopped him short.

Frank noticed the stunned expression on his brother's face. "What is it?"

Joe held up a small framed photograph that showed a grinning Eli Travers with his arm around Jessica Albright.

Frank moved in for a closer look. "So she did lie," he said. "She knew Eli before he came to Langston."

"And pretty well, from the looks of this," Joe said.

Frank picked up the phone. "I think it's time for another chat with Jessica."

He reached her at the S.A.C. office.

"Jessica, this is Frank Hardy. We need to speak to you in person for a couple of minutes. It's important."

"I'm sorry, Frank, but I'm really busy. Can't we do it over the phone?"

"It's about Eli Travers."

"The kidnapping?"

"That's right. We have certain evidence that may implicate you. I'd rather not say anything more over the phone."

There was a brief pause, then Jessica said, "Okay, fine. Meet me at the Student Union snack shop in ten minutes."

Jessica was waiting in a booth when they got there. She was holding a torn paper napkin in both hands, and a pile of shredded paper lay on the table in front of her. Frank and Joe sat down across from her.

"Jessica, you've got to tell the truth," Frank said. "How long have you known Eli?"

"About five months. We met last spring at a student government summit in Washington and kind of fell for each other. That's why he transferred here."

"So why keep it a secret from us?" Joe asked.

"At first I didn't want my father to find out Eli was here. He met Eli last spring and didn't approve of him."

"Eli was involved in protests against U.S. involvement in Gabiz, wasn't he?" Joe said.

Jessica nodded. "Dad thought he was some kind of traitor and told me not to see him. I was afraid he'd flip out if he knew Eli had transferred here. But I was terrified when you told me Eli had been kidnapped."

She let out a sigh and blew a few bits of shredded napkin across the table. "So I told my father all about the kidnapping, right before you came to my house yesterday," she said with a glance at Frank. "He didn't take the news very well. And he didn't think I should tell you."

"Why not?" Joe asked.

"He said I should talk to the police if I had something to contribute. If I didn't, I should just keep quiet. He said that was the only way to deal with a kidnapping. Any outside interference like what you guys are doing could endanger Eli and hinder the efforts of the police. I guess his military background has taught him to follow official channels and act only under orders from superiors. I really didn't know anything that would help the police find Eli, so I followed Dad's orders. But I've been so worried."

Frank noticed she was close to tears. "It's okay, Jessica," he said. "You did the right thing. I don't see how your relationship with Eli affects the case at this point. But you understand we have to be concerned if someone's not telling us the truth."

Jessica took a few moments to regain her composure. "I'm really sorry I lied to you guys," she said. "I hope you understand it was for all the right reasons. Now I've got to go. Please call me right away if you need anything or if you hear any news of Eli. And I do appreciate your efforts to find him." She stood up and walked out.

As Frank and Joe got up to leave, Joe said, "I believe her."

"So do I," Frank said. "But where does it leave us? I guess we just have to keep after Nye and Shapley and be on the lookout for anything else that might crop up."

When they got back to the dorm, Joe gave Amos Thorpe a call to see what kind of progress the private investigator had made.

"Not much," Thorpe said. "I started surveillance on Nye and Shapley, but they were onto me almost as fast as you guys were. I guess I just stick out too much on a college campus."

Joe told him they were going to keep watch and would let him know if they got any results.

Since the two thugs already knew the Hardys' van, Frank and Joe borrowed Richie's white compact.

They parked down the street from Nye and Shapley's house, about a five-minute drive from Richie's dorm. The house was a one-floor cinder-block rental with peeling paint and a car seat on the front porch. The green van was gone, so Frank and Joe settled in to wait.

Nye and Shapley showed up at dusk and carried a couple of bags from a fast-food restaurant into the house. A few minutes later the Hardys could see a television come on in the living room.

"Oh, boy," Joe said, "it looks like culture night at the Nye and Shapley household."

He broke out some sandwiches he and Frank had picked up earlier that afternoon. Frank ate half his sandwich, then lay back in his seat to get some rest. He and Joe would watch the house in shifts, all night if necessary.

It wasn't. Shortly before midnight, the lights went off in the house. Frank was on watch, and Joe was taking his turn to nap. Frank figured Nye and Shapley had gone to bed, but he was paying close attention anyway, just in case.

Frank's watchfulness paid off ten minutes later when he caught sight of a pair of shadows slipping from the house to the van. A few seconds later the van pulled out. Its headlights didn't come on until it was two blocks away.

Frank started Richie's compact and followed. As the car began to move, Joe sat up and yelled, "Hey, wait a minute!"

Frank looked over at him quizzically.

Joe blinked for a few seconds, then remembered where he was. "Sorry about that," he said, "but the last time I woke up in a moving vehicle, it was the van and it almost dumped me into a river."

"I'll try not to let that happen with this car," Frank said, gazing straight ahead. He was concentrating on keeping Nye and Shapley's van in sight without getting too close.

After about twenty minutes of following in silence, Joe said, "Looks like they're headed for the incinerator site." But several minutes later the green van took a side road, ruining that theory. Joe got out a map and a penlight and tracked their progress until Nye and Shapley finally pulled into a county picnic area.

Frank drove a hundred yards past them, then slowed to a crawl just long enough for Joe to hop out. Frank drove another half mile, then doubled back and coasted into the parking lot with his headlights off.

Joe appeared at the window as soon as Frank rolled to a stop. "They headed down a trail over there," Joe said, pointing into the woods.

"Good," Frank said, checking the map with his penlight. "It looks as if the incinerator site is less than a mile from here."

"Let's go," Joe said. He reached into the backseat for their camera, which was equipped with infrared film and a zoom lens. Maybe they could snap a few photos of Nye and Shapley sabotaging the construction site. That ought to be enough evidence for the authorities to arrest them.

Frank and Joe followed Nye and Shapley's trail. After half an hour of moving quietly through the darkened woods, they emerged on a hilltop. At the bottom of the grassy slope they could see Nye and Shapley scaling the high fence that surrounded the incinerator site.

"Where are Thorpe's security guys?" Joe whispered.

"They probably make timed rounds. As soon as they come by, we can tip them off."

Being careful to keep a safe distance, the Hardys followed Nye and Shapley over the fence and continued to track them. They could see the skeleton of one of the incinerator buildings—big steel supports on a concrete base—looming ahead. Using piles of excavated earth for cover, Frank and Joe maneuvered closer until they saw Nye and Shapley hunched at the base of the structure. Joe snapped a few photos, but Nye and Shapley were huddled over so that he couldn't make out what they were doing.

Nye and Shapley went deeper into the structure, and Frank and Joe moved in. A coffee can was taped to one of the steel columns. Frank shone his penlight into the can.

"Is that what I think it is?" Joe asked.

"Another bomb," Frank whispered. "We've got almost an hour before it goes off."

"Look," Joe muttered. "There's that same red wire I found in the—"

Something big hit Joe from behind, knocking him headfirst into one of the columns. As his forehead thudded against the steel, he went limp and collapsed on the concrete flooring.

Frank spun around and saw Dale Shapley looming over him with a piece of steel pipe in his hand. Frank looked from Shapley to Joe. He wanted to check on his brother, but he couldn't afford to turn his back on Shapley.

"If you hurt him," Frank said in a low, even voice, "I'll—"

"You won't do anything," Shapley said with a crooked grin. "Because right now it's pay-back time." He raised the steel pipe high over his shoulder, preparing to smash it into Frank's head.

Chapter

10

FRANK DUCKED as Shapley swung the pipe at his head. It clanged off the column, and Frank moved in quickly, punching Shapley in his solar plexus, which dropped him to his hands and knees and left him gasping for air.

A brick flew past Frank's ear and smashed to a pile of dust on the concrete floor. He turned to see a figure ducking into the shadows about twenty feet away. Frank chased him and was gaining on him when the other guy suddenly fell to the ground with a scream. Frank saw that the man was Nye, twisting in agony as he clutched his right foot. He had stepped in a drainage trough.

"Oh, man. My ankle," Nye wailed. "I think it's broken."

Frank, thinking about what the brick would have done to his head, couldn't muster much sympathy. Nye wasn't going anywhere on that ankle, so Frank went back to Joe, who was beginning to stir.

Joe probed at his forehead, winced, and groaned. "Did that bomb go off?" he asked.

"No," Frank said. "How many fingers am I holding up?"

"Three, Coach. Can I go back in the game now?"

"Sorry, game's over," Frank told him. "Nye's got a broken ankle, and Shapley—"

He looked over to where he had left Shapley struggling for breath, but he was gone.

"He got away," Frank said. "Watch Nye. I'll—"

Several shouts echoed from the far end of the structure. Then a pair of powerful flashlight beams cut through the darkness, and two security guards jogged over to Nye.

"They can take care of Nye," Joe said. "Let's go after the big guy."

Frank and Joe ran back toward the spot where they had climbed the fence. As they approached it, they could make out Shapley's silhouette dropping down on the other side and lumbering back up the hillside.

Frank and Joe were clambering up the fence when Frank saw Shapley stop, turn, and heave something in their direction. The object arced out of the darkness, landed on the hillside, and rolled down toward them. It was another coffee can.

"Get down," Frank yelled, dropping back off the fence and sprinting in the opposite direction. Joe followed, and they took cover behind an earth mound. A second later a thunderous explosion rocked the ground around them, followed by a rain of dirt and gravel.

Frank and Joe stood up and shook off the debris. Between them and the fence, the bomb had carved out a shallow crater about two feet deep and twelve feet across. The pair of flashlights converged on them, and one of the security guards shouted, "Freeze! We've got you covered."

Frank and Joe surrendered and waited for the guards to call Amos Thorpe and the police. Once Thorpe arrived, it took another twenty-five minutes to sort out the whole story. Nye was taken to the hospital to have his ankle set, the security men called in an expert, who helped them defuse the first bomb, and a police unit was dispatched to the picnic area to check for Shapley's van, but by that time it was gone.

Thorpe asked Frank and Joe to meet him at the police station. They waited in an interrogation room with Detective Loomis until Nye was brought back from the hospital. He hobbled in on crutches, his ankle in a fresh cast, the leg of his jeans slit up to the knee.

"Have a seat, Mr. Nye," Detective Loomis said. "Do you understand exactly how much trouble you are in?"

"I guess so," Nye said sullenly. He eased himself into a chair across from the others and laid his crutches across his lap.

"Do you?" Loomis continued. "Detonating explosive devices with the intent to damage government property—that alone could put you behind bars until that ponytail of yours turns gray. You've also got vandalism, arson, kidnapping, attempted murder—"

"Wait a second," Nye said. "Look, I admit we were going to set off a few bombs at the incinerator, and we damaged some stuff up there, but we never tried to kidnap or kill anybody."

"Sure, pal," Loomis said. "The problem is, you're the only suspect we have in custody right now."

"It's true. I wouldn't lie to you," Nye insisted. "Look, I'll tell you everything. Maybe we can work out a deal if I cooperate, okay? It was all Dale's fault anyway. He's the one who always took things too far. He's the one you should be locking up."

So much for *that* partnership, Frank thought.

Nye began a detailed account of their activities. He told the police which nights he and Dale had gone up to the site, how they had gotten in each time, and what acts they had committed. When he got up to the bombing that night, Joe interrupted him.

"Where did you get the bombs?"

"We made them," Nye said.

"At the old airfield, right?" Joe said. "So where did you learn how to make them?"

Nye looked surprised. "We met this guy at Dizzy Liz's about a month ago. Dale was shooting his mouth off. This guy overheard him, and we started talking. He said he admired the strength of our beliefs and wanted to help us."

"This guy have a name?" Thorpe asked.

"Mr. Williams. That's all he ever told us. I don't know how to find him or get in touch with him. Maybe Dale does. Mr. Williams usually found *us*."

"Was this Mr. Williams at the Quonset hut yesterday when you were putting the finishing touches on your coffee-can bombs?" Joe asked.

"He stopped by to look things over, and then he told us we had to clear out of there because somebody had found the place and was snooping around."

Frank caught a meaningful look from Joe. Mr. Williams had to be the one who had almost strangled Joe, then handcuffed him to the van and sent it rolling down the hill. After he took care of Joe, he must have gone back to the airfield to warn Nye and Shapley. The two thugs would never have known Joe was spying on them if it hadn't been for their friend Williams.

"This Mr. Williams," Frank said. "Did he ever ask you to do anything for him?"

Nye shook his head. "He said he might need our help for an operation of his own, but he never said what it was or anything else about it."

"Did he borrow Shapley's van the day Eli Travers was kidnapped?" Joe asked.

Nye licked his lips and glanced down at his crutches. "I don't know."

"But he could have?" Frank prompted him.

"Yes," Nye said. "He knows where we live and that Dale always leaves the key in the van. When you came around saying the van had been used in a kidnapping, he was the first one I thought of."

"Nice of you to tell us," Loomis said. "So what does this Mr. Williams look like?"

"Just a regular guy, in his midthirties, I guess. Short dark hair, medium height and build."

"You're going to have to be a little more specific than that," Thorpe said.

"I don't know. . . ." Nye said. He thought about it for a moment, then held up his hands. "There's nothing that jumps out about him. Really. I mean, he's the kind of guy you don't look at twice."

They grilled Nye for another ten minutes, but the rest of the interrogation didn't yield anything significant. When it was over, the Hardys thanked Thorpe and Loomis for including them and headed back to the dorm to catch up on their sleep.

When he finally dozed off, Joe dreamed of a blank-faced man choking him from behind. He woke the next morning with a start, convinced somebody had just thrown another coffee-can bomb at him.

"Whoa!" Joe said.

Richie glanced over at him and whispered, "Hey, keep it down, I'm trying to study." He was propped up on his pillows in bed, reading a comic book.

Frank, asleep on the floor between them in his sleeping bag, clutched his pillow, muttered, and rolled over.

"So what happened last night?" Richie asked. "You guys were out way past my bedtime."

Joe filled him in. "They've got an APB out on Shapley and his van," he said. "And we've got a suspect with a name—Mr. Williams—but not much of a description. Frank and I figured we'd go check out Dizzy Liz's and some of Nye and Shapley's other hangouts to see if we can spot him."

"That sounds like a long shot," Richie said. "Why do you think this Williams guy would kidnap Eli?"

Joe shrugged. "Usually it's for the ransom, but there hasn't been any demand, which is strange. Maybe something happened between Eli and this Williams guy. The thing is, as Frank was saying, this Mr. Williams and whoever he's working with have some skills— bomb building, martial arts, hand-to-hand combat. They definitely know what they're doing. And they're going to be tough to track down."

"Then you could use some help, right?" Richie said. "Today's Saturday, and classes haven't even started yet. I know a lot of guys with time on their hands. If we give them a description of the guy and assign them places to hang out, we'll have a much better chance of nailing him."

"I wish we had a decent description," Joe said. "There must be several thousand medium-size, mid-thirtyish men with dark hair in his town."

"True," came Frank's groggy voice as he boosted himself up on one elbow, "but it's worth a shot. A lot of these places are hangouts for college kids. If he comes back to one of them, he should be pretty easy to pick out. Or if he tries to recruit people, maybe they could give us a lead on him."

"Somehow, I don't think he's going to expose himself the way Thorpe did," Joe said. "But you're right, Frank, we've got to give it a try and hope we come up with a lead. I'm going to grab a shower. I'll be ready in ten minutes."

Joe got some soap and a towel and headed for the door. When he pulled it open, he was surprised to see a man with short blond hair, wearing a dark suit and dark sunglasses, standing right on the threshold. Joe found himself staring at his own reflection in the man's glasses for a second. The man, who was about six feet two, stood stock-still with his feet slightly apart and his arms clasped behind his back.

"May I help you?" Joe asked.

"I'm looking for Frank Hardy, Joe Hardy, and Richie Simmons," the man stated in a flat, businesslike voice.

Joe nodded. "That's us."

"All right," the man said. "Would you please come with us?"

Joe turned quickly and said, "Hey, Richie, are you expecting—" But before he could finish, the man grabbed Joe's arm just above the wrist and said, "Come on. Let's go."

Joe's shampoo and soap case clattered to the floor. "Hey, get off of me," he said, and twisted his arm loose. But the man shoved Joe back into the room with both hands.

Suddenly six more men in dark suits barged in as the first man gestured at Frank and Richie. "Let's go, fellows. No point in putting up a fight. If you do that, somebody will get hurt."

Chapter

11

JOE BOUNCED BACK and kicked the first man in the chest, sending him reeling into the closet doors. His dark glasses clattered to the floor. Two others quickly grabbed Joe's arms and pinned him up against the wall.

The rest of them yanked Frank and Richie out of bed and dragged them into the hallway. The one Joe had kicked got to his feet and picked up his glasses.

"So you're a tough guy, huh?" the man said, pressing his face close to Joe's.

"Whenever I get a chance," Joe said. With the two men holding his arms, he swung up both legs and kicked the man again, sending him flying across the room. This time the man's glasses flew off and hit the wall—the lenses popped out.

"That's it," the man said. He reached into his suit coat and pulled out a black plastic device with two shiny steel probes on one end. "Know what this is, tough guy?"

Joe didn't answer. The man flicked a switch and a brilliant jag of electricity crackled between the steel probes.

"This is twelve thousand bolts of pure agony," the man said. "Just give me an excuse to use it, smart-mouth. I'm begging you."

The two men holding Joe dragged him out of the room by the arms. He wanted to make a break for it, but he knew that a dose from that stun gun would definitely ruin his day.

The men hustled the Hardys and Richie out of the dorm and tossed all three of them into the back of a waiting limousine. A glass partition separated them from the driver and the other man in the front seat.

"The door handles don't work," Joe said as the limo got under way.

"What is this? What's going on?" Richie asked. "Who *are* these guys?"

"Just relax and enjoy the ride, Richie," Frank said, checking to see if there was anything inside the limousine's mini-refrigerator. "It's not going to help if we panic."

After a short drive, the limo slipped up to

the rear door of the Langston Luxury Hotel. The grim men in suits shoved the Hardys inside to a service elevator. When one of them pressed a button, Frank tried to see which floor he hit, but the man shielded the panel with his body. Another had his hand pressed to an earpiece. Frank noticed he also had a transmitter mike on his lapel.

When the elevator doors opened, the man with the earpiece got out. As he strode down the hallway, he cocked his head and said something into his mike. The other man pointed, and they followed the first man to a room where two more dark-suited men stood guard. One of the guards opened the door, and Frank, Joe, and Richie were motioned in without a word. Their three escorts remained outside.

The room was comfortably furnished with plush sofas and chairs in neutral colors. The blinds on the windows were almost completely shut, and it was gloomy. They smelled fresh bacon and then noticed that muffins, coffee, and covered dishes were laid out on a table surrounded by four chairs. Seeing the breakfast setup made Joe realize how hungry he was.

Just then someone stepped in from the adjoining bedroom, snapped on the lights, and said, "Good morning, young men."

It was General Albright. He was dressed informally, in a dark polo shirt and slacks, but there was no mistaking his military bearing.

The general looked the three of them over. They felt out of place, standing there in their gym shorts and T-shirts. Joe barely concealed a scowl, and Richie's eyes were bulging in amazement.

"Why don't you three help yourselves to some breakfast?" the general said, waving them over to the table. "My daughter told me about your efforts to find her ... ah ... friend Eli. I'm eager to hear about your progress."

"So you had your storm troopers drag us over here?" Joe said.

The general cleared his throat and stepped closer to Joe. "Did they ruffle your feathers a little bit, son?" he said. "Sometimes they take their job too seriously. But they're my men, and I take full responsibility for them. Will you accept my sincere apology?"

"Yes, sir," Joe said, stiffening under the general's scrutiny. "That bacon sure smells good, sir."

"So dig in," the general said with a chuckle.

He joined the Hardys and Richie at the table and helped himself to a tumbler of orange juice.

"You're keeping up on Eli's case, General Albright?" Frank asked as he filled a plate with scrambled eggs and hash browns.

"That's right," he said. "I've offered my resources to help the investigation, and I'm staying in personal touch with the local authorities. Which reminds me, there was a development early this morning."

"What was that?" Joe asked. He stopped to wipe his fingers on his napkin. He had just finished putting together a large sandwich of scrambled eggs and bacon on toast.

"The authorities picked Shapley up as he was trying to cross the border into Canada," the general said. "He had high-quality forged ID."

"If the ID was so good, how did they catch him?" Frank asked. "Did they recognize the van?"

The general shook his head. "My people faxed a photo and description of him to various agencies. An alert border guard recognized Shapley. He was driving a car rented with a stolen credit card from an agency about thirty miles from here. They still haven't found his van."

As they continued to discuss the case, Joe started to warm up to the man. He seemed to have the general enthralled as he told him about their adventures so far at Langston.

Frank stayed quiet, however. It was fascinating for him to see how the canny statesman seemed to coax every detail out of Joe while asking hardly any direct questions. It occurred to Frank why they were really here: the general wanted to know how much they knew and what they intended to do.

Then Frank realized something else. The mysterious Mr. Williams, with his martial arts and demolitions skills, sounded like someone who had been trained by a government intelligence agency. Of all the people they had spoken to, only the general, who disapproved of Eli seeing his daughter and who considered him a traitor for protesting American involvement in Gabiz, had a strong reason to dislike the kidnapped student.

Could the general have sent one of his agents—"Mr. Williams"—to buddy up with Nye and Shapley and frame them for kidnapping Eli? That was a little far-fetched, especially since Mr. Williams seemed to be helping Nye and Shapley build bombs to use against the incinerator, which the general supported. Maybe Williams had just gotten carried away, Frank thought. Hadn't the general himself just apologized for some of his agents who had taken his orders too far?

Frank tried to keep up his end of the conversation, but at the same time he kept his eye on the general and he kept turning over all the possibilities in his mind.

* * *

During the limo ride back to the dorm, Frank told Joe and Richie about his speculations.

"I've got to admit," Joe said, "that without any ransom demand, the fact that the general doesn't like Eli is the only real motive we've come up with so far."

As soon as they got back to the dorm, Richie and the Hardys went ahead with their plan to recruit other students to check Nye and Shapley's haunts in their manhunt for Mr. Williams. First they made a list of possible hangouts; then they called Jessica, who suggested a few more.

Next they held a meeting with the twenty "agents" Richie had rounded up. They assigned a two-person team to each location. Frank, Joe, and Richie went to Dizzy Liz's. The Hardys took the cellular phone from their van. As soon as one of their agents saw a person matching Williams's description or got any kind of lead on him, he was supposed to call it in.

It was a long day, with several possible leads, none of which went anywhere. Joe spent most of the afternoon following a man who had stopped in Dizzy Liz's for coffee. He turned out to be a salesman who had been in California at the time of Eli's kidnapping. That was the closest they got.

They didn't give it up until almost midnight. When they got back to the dorm, all they could think about was getting some sleep and starting over in the morning.

A lanky young man in muddy boots, jeans, and a flannel shirt was sitting on the floor in the hallway, leaning against the door to Richie's room. His plastic-framed glasses had slipped down his nose, and he was snoring.

Richie nudged him with the toe of his shoe. "Jeb," he said, "what's the matter? Couldn't find your room? It's down the hall."

Jeb stopped in mid-snore and blinked up at them, disoriented. He pushed his glasses up his nose and stood up slowly. "It's about time you got back, Richie," he said.

"Frank, Joe," Richie said, "this is Jeb Clancy. He's an entomology major. He would have been helping us, but he has a job working for some farmers, counting bugs out in the fields or something. What's up, Jeb?"

Jeb was still blinking the sleep out of his eyes, but there was excitement in his voice. "I found that van I heard you were looking for," he said.

"What?" Richie said.

"You know, the green one that Eli's kidnapper used."

Chapter

12

FRANK COULD HARDLY BELIEVE IT. They had just spent the whole day chasing all over town in search of a lead, and it was waiting on their doorstep when they got back to the dorm.

"Where is it?" Joe asked.

"On the property of an old closed-down quarry about fifteen miles from here," Jeb said. "One of the farmers I worked for today was complaining about it. You couldn't see it from the road, he said, but you could from a hill on his property. I didn't get there until dusk, so I couldn't see anything, but he swore it was there, an old green van parked where he hadn't seen a car in years."

"Did he see any people?" Frank asked.

"No," Jeb said. "He said the van was there in the morning, and he kept checking on it all day, but he didn't see anyone. He was afraid someone had bought the property and was going to build there. It's his favorite hunting spot."

"Great," Joe said. "So how do we find this place?"

Jeb gave them directions and then headed down the hall to get some sleep.

"It looks like we're in for another late night," Frank said. The brothers weren't thrilled at the prospect of missing more sleep, but they were excited to have a break in the case.

The Hardys and Richie took their black van and followed Jeb's directions deep into the hilly country north of the university. They almost missed the turnoff to the quarry. It was a narrow road, and the pavement was all broken up into big angled slabs, like ice floes, except that these slabs had weeds growing up through the cracks.

"I don't know about this," Frank said as he made the turn.

"It has to be the right road," Joe said, checking the map again. "It's the only turnoff for miles."

"Man, it doesn't look as if anyone's been here in this century," Frank said as he carefully maneuvered along the bucking, heaving pavement.

After a quarter mile, they came to a clearing. In the middle of it they could see the foundation of a collapsed building. Nye and Shapley's van was parked next to the foundation. The road continued past it but was blocked by a fallen tree.

Frank parked and the three of them climbed out. Joe went over to the van.

"This is it, all right," he said.

Frank walked around behind the van to check out the other side of the ruins. He found a motorcycle parked off in the shadows of the underbrush. He held his hand down next to the engine—it was still hot.

"Hey, Frank, do you think—" Joe was saying as he walked around the van to join his brother.

Frank clamped a hand over his brother's mouth and nodded at the motorcycle. "The engine's still warm," he whispered. "It looks like somebody's around here. It could be Mr. Williams."

"What do we do?" Richie asked as the three of them huddled together.

"I want to look around and see what he's up to," Joe said.

"Me, too," Frank said. "But we should call

Mike DeFinis first and get some cops out here. One of us should stay here and wait for them."

They looked at Richie, whose eyes suddenly got huge. "Me?" he said. "Are you out of your minds? I'm not sitting here in the dark waiting for some bomb-building ninja kidnapper to sneak up and strangle me."

"Just lock yourself in our van," Frank told him. "If he comes back before we do, start honking the horn like crazy."

Richie thought about it for a couple of seconds, then let out a big sigh. "Okay, okay," he whispered. "I suppose one of us has to be the hero."

Frank went back to the van and made a call to the police station from the cellular phone. Officer DeFinis told him the county police could have officers there in fifteen minutes. Then the Hardys left Richie in the van and headed farther down the road, past the fallen tree. The pavement was almost completely overgrown with trees and bushes, but they were able to follow it for a few hundred yards until it ended at the edge of the quarry.

When they got to the edge, the quarry opened up in front of them. It was bigger than a dozen football fields and so deep they couldn't see the bottom in the darkness. A rocky ramp hugged its side wall and wound down into the black depths below. Rough gravel tracks led in both directions around the quarry's edge.

"What do you think?" Joe asked.

"Let's circle around the top and see if we can find anything before the cops get here," Frank said. "When they get here, we can check out the bottom."

"Okay," Joe said. "You go left, I'll go right, and we'll meet on the far side."

Frank started out along the gravel path to the left. He came across the rusting hulk of an abandoned dump truck after a few minutes and continued on. The forest had grown back almost to the edge of the quarry in places. He had to pick his way carefully through the underbrush so as not to slip on the crumbling stone and fall off the edge.

He was thinking he should be running into Joe soon when he reached another small clearing. In its center a flat-footed shack of rusted sheet metal stood at a strange angle, as if frozen in the act of collapsing. Frank hesitated, thinking maybe he should wait for Joe before checking it out, but he decided Joe would be along any minute anyway. He picked out the door of the shack in the dim starlight and pulled it open.

At first he couldn't make out anything in the dark. He was reaching for his penlight when he heard a slight rustling.

Frank started to back away. Then something hit him in the face, and stars exploded in his eyes. Someone sprang out of the shack as Frank staggered back several steps, trying to clear his head. All he could see was a shadow in the darkness. Before he could react, a well-aimed kick caught Frank flush in the chest and knocked him backward again, right over the edge of an enormous pit.

Joe was moving fast along the trail. He hadn't seen anything so far, and he was getting impatient. It was so dark where the forest met the quarry that he thought he could have passed an army without seeing it.

Then he heard a shout from up ahead and recognized Frank's voice. He charged ahead as fast as he could without running into a tree.

When he reached the ramshackle shed in the clearing, he shouted, "Hey, Frank!"

"Down here," came his brother's voice from the depths of the quarry. Even though the quarry was huge, Frank's voice seemed surprisingly close.

Joe stepped to the edge and peered down into the darkness. He could make out his brother's face, grimacing with the effort of clinging to a ledge a dozen feet down.

"Hang on, Frank," Joe said. "I'll be right there."

They'd both been rock climbing many times, but usually with the proper equipment and in broad daylight. Climbing the chiseled side of the quarry in darkness was something else entirely. Joe lowered himself over the edge and scrambled down to the ledge where Frank was hanging.

"Okay," Joe said, "I'm going to reach down and grab your hand. See if you can find a toe-hold—"

The ledge collapsed under Joe's feet. His fingers grazed Frank's hand, and then he was plunging out of control through the darkness. Joe felt a surge of terror as he realized he was about to die. He let out a scream, but it was cut short seconds later when he hit cold water. He propelled himself to the surface and heard Frank splashing nearby.

"Nice save," Frank called sarcastically as they swam closer. "Did you know the quarry was flooded before you dropped us in here?"

"Sure, Frank," Joe said. "It was all part of my brilliant master plan."

They swam to the far side of the quarry, where the water turned out to be only about three feet deep. Lucky we didn't take the plunge over here, Joe thought. They found the bottom of the winding ramp that circled the quarry. As they trudged toward the top, Frank said, "When I found that shack by the edge of the quarry, there was somebody in there. He waited till I got right up to the door. Then, when I opened it, he smacked me in the face and kicked me over the edge. This guy isn't messing around."

"Do you think it was Williams?" Joe asked.

"Might have been," Frank said. "It was too dark. I never got a good look at him."

By the time they made it back to Richie, the police had arrived and the motorcycle was gone.

"Didn't you hear me honking?" Richie asked. "I started as soon as I heard the motorcycle, but he just rode off. Hey, you guys are all wet."

Frank and Joe explained what had happened. Then they led the officers back to the shack where Frank had been attacked. When they shone their flashlights around inside, the beams fell on a pale figure curled up motionless on the dirt floor.

"It's Eli!" Richie said. His wrists and ankles were bound, and the floor around him was littered with disposable syringes and empty vials.

One of the police officers immediately radioed for an ambulance. Frank bent over Eli, checked for a pulse on his neck, then pulled back his eyelids to look at his pupils.

"He's alive," Frank said. "Just barely."

"Looks like an overdose," the second officer said. "I don't think he has much time."

Frank snatched Eli up in a fireman's carry and hurried out of the shack with him, followed by the others.

"The ambulance is never going to find us back here," the first officer said as they reached their cars. "We'll have to take him straight to Angel of Mercy if he's going to have any chance."

The officer opened the back door of his cruiser, and Joe helped Frank put Eli inside. Richie climbed in the other side.

"We'll meet you at the hospital," Frank said. Then the cruiser took off into the night, lights flashing and siren wailing.

"Did you notice the labels on those vials?" Joe asked.

Frank shook his head. "No. Let's go back and check. They may need to know at the hospital."

The hurried back to the shack. Using their penlights, they searched the floor and gathered up all the empty vials.

Frank read from the labels. "Sedanil. Must be some kind of sedative." He went back to their van and called in the information to the hospital.

Meanwhile, Joe kept searching around the room. When Frank got back, Joe held up a small key and said, "Look at this. I found it by the door." Frank moved in for a closer look. The key had a laminated tag that said "Storage City, 24-Hour Self-Storage, Units of All Sizes." The number 113 was stamped on the key.

"Our friend Mr. Williams probably dropped this when he jumped me," Frank said.

They checked the shack once more, inside and out, but couldn't find anything else. Then they hopped in the van and headed back to town, putting in a call to Officer DeFinis on the way. He gave them the address of Storage City and said he'd meet them there.

Storage City was a large fenced compound tucked between a hotel and a waffle house on a Langston thoroughfare packed with franchise businesses. When the Hardys pulled up, they saw a police cruiser parked by the office. The night manager buzzed them through the main gate, checked their IDs, and then took them inside the office, where Mike DeFinis was waiting.

"I just got here a couple of minutes ago," DeFinis said. "It seems unit one-thirteen was rented two weeks ago to a Mr. William Stone."

They thanked the manager, went out to the parking lot, and followed the signs down a well-lighted lane between long, low buildings lined with garage-type doors until they found unit 113. DeFinis pulled out his flashlight and shone it on the door. Joe got out the key and opened the lock. When he and Frank bent down and pulled up on the door, it made a loud rattling sound as it went up. The storage unit was empty except for a long freezer whose hum echoed off the metal walls and concrete floor.

"This is weird," Joe muttered. "Why would someone lease storage space just for a freezer?"

"Let's check it out," Frank said. He stepped up to the freezer, grabbed the handle, and pulled it open. Frank, Joe, and Officer DeFinis leaned over, and in the eerie glow of the flashlight, stared open-mouthed at the gruesome contents.

Wrapped tightly in a large transparent plastic bag, and staring up at them through the frost with lifeless, wide-open eyes, was a dark-haired man with a mustache.

Chapter

13

"OKAY, GUYS," the officer said, breaking the stunned silence. "Let's go call this one in."

Frank slowly closed the lid of the freezer and turned to follow Joe and the officer back to the cruiser.

Joe felt a shiver despite the warmth of the night. He knew it would be a long time before he could get the sight of the frozen corpse out of his mind.

Detective Loomis, along with a squad from the coroner's office, arrived at Storage City's unit 113 within ten minutes of Officer DeFinis's radio call. After scanning the crime scene, the detective joined the Hardys beside their van.

"Were you able to ID him?" Frank asked after the detective had taken down their statements.

"No," the detective said. "His pockets are clean—no wallet, no personal effects. He's not even wearing a watch."

"Any idea whether he was killed first and then frozen or . . ." Joe asked.

"Or just locked in there alive?" Loomis said. "There's no way of telling at this point. There aren't any obvious wounds. The body's frozen solid, so it's been in there at least twenty-four hours. The coroner can't do an autopsy until it thaws. Even then, because of the freezing, it'll be virtually impossible to determine time of death."

"This is getting frustrating," Joe said. "First a kidnapping, then a murder, and nothing but a bunch of dead-end leads."

"You got Eli back alive," Loomis said. "That counts for a lot in my book. Now, why don't you just let us handle the rest of this while you kids lie low and try to stay out of trouble?"

"If there's anything else we can do . . ." Joe said.

"Thanks, but no thanks," Loomis said. "Now if you'll excuse me, I need to get back to work here."

"All right. So long, Detective," Frank said. "And good luck with the investigation."

"We've got to track down this Mr. Williams," Joe said as they got in the van.

Frank nodded his head. "Eli is just one piece of the puzzle. So is the dead guy in the freezer. But how do they fit together? That's the question."

They headed to the hospital, where they met Richie in the waiting room. Eli was officially in stable condition. The doctors had been able to counteract the sedative overdose with stimulants; he'd be sleeping it off for a while, though.

Next they went back to the dorm with Richie, hoping to catch a few hours' sleep and make sense of the case in the morning.

They all slept late the next morning, ate a big breakfast, and made it to the hospital just before noon. They found Jessica Albright in the waiting room, tearing a brochure into pieces and absentmindedly throwing them into a wastebasket.

"How is Eli?" Frank asked Jessica.

"They haven't let me see him yet," she said. "He's still asleep. One of the nurses has promised to let me know as soon as he wakes up."

"How did you know he was here?" Frank

asked, feeling bad about not calling her himself.

"My father found out and let me know," she said. "He's been a big help. He was going to come down and wait with me, but he has this important reception at the university president's house in a couple of hours. I told him I'd be okay. I was glad he offered, though."

A nurse came in and told them Eli was awake. "You can spend a few minutes with him, but that's all," she said. "He still needs a lot of rest."

The four of them followed her to Eli's room and found him propped up on several pillows. He was looking forlornly at a tray of hospital food that was laid out in front of him.

"Hey, visitors," Eli said. "All right!"

Jessica went over and gave Eli a hug. Richie introduced Frank and Joe.

"Thanks, guys," he said. "You saved my life. I don't even remember what happened. All I know is that guy who was pretending to be Professor Rocco kept me so drugged I couldn't see straight."

"Hold it right there," Frank said. "What do you mean, the guy pretending to be Professor Rocco?"

"The one who kidnapped me and locked me up in that shed," Eli said. "Didn't you nail him?"

"Not exactly," Joe said.

"You're saying that an impostor is posing at your professor?" Jessica said.

"That's right," Eli said. "I dropped by his office in the geology building to say hi, but when I got there, I found some other guy sitting behind his desk. He looked a lot like Professor Rocco—same hair and mustache and everything—so I was a little freaked out at first."

"Then what happened?" Joe asked.

"I said I was looking for Professor Rocco, that I was a friend of his from Amberlin. The man behind the desk said he was Professor Simon from down the hall and he was using Rocco's phone because his was out of order. He said Rocco was out to lunch, but he'd pass on my address and phone number so Rocco could call me."

"Which let the impostor know exactly where to find you," Frank said.

"He had to get you out of the way before you figured out he was an impostor," Joe said. "So he borrowed Shapley's van. He's our Mr. Williams—or at least somebody working with him. Once he got the van, he just waited for you to turn up at the dorm, and then he grabbed you."

Eli blinked at them. "But why is he posing

as Professor Rocco? And where's the real Rocco?"

Frank thought it was too soon to tell Eli about the mustached man they'd found in the freezer at Storage City. Besides, they'd have to wait for the autopsy for positive proof that it was Rocco.

The door opened, and Detective Loomis walked in. "Okay, anybody who wasn't kidnapped, out of the room," he said. "We've got some questions to ask Eli."

The Hardys and Richie filed out of the room. "I'll come back as soon as they let me," Jessica said to Eli before following them out.

"I say we go check out Rocco's office," Joe said.

"Let's do it," Frank said.

They left Richie and Jessica at the hospital and headed back to the campus.

"So our kidnapper killed Rocco, put the body on ice in Storage City, and then took his place," Joe said on the way over. "Wouldn't somebody have recognized him as an impostor?"

"Rocco just transferred here," Frank said. "If the impostor looked like him or had a decent disguise, nobody would have noticed the difference."

"Somebody had to have met Rocco," Joe said. "How about the person who hired him?"

Frank turned to face Joe, who was behind the wheel. "Like maybe the dean of science," Frank said.

"Who conveniently died in a car accident last week," Joe said. "Do you think—"

"That they would have arranged a fatal accident for the dean just so this guy could pose as Rocco?" Frank finished Joe's thought. "Maybe. If they did, they're either totally vicious or totally cold and calculating."

"Or all of the above," Joe said. "Their plan is pretty well thought through."

"Except they didn't count on Eli's turning up here at Langston," Frank said.

"True, but they dealt with it," Joe said. "They kept their cool, came up with a plan to kidnap Eli, and executed it within a couple of hours."

"Williams may be quick with a punch, but he made a mistake," Frank said. "He dumped the van too close to the place where he stashed Eli. If it hadn't been for Jeb's farmer friend, the van might still be sitting out there, and so would Eli."

"I wonder why they bothered to keep Eli alive," Joe said. "They didn't bother with the dean of science or Professor Rocco."

"Good question," Frank said. "I can't wait to ask Williams myself—if we ever catch up to him, that is."

They found the geology building open but mostly empty, as was to be expected on a Sunday afternoon. On their way up to Rocco's office on the third floor, they saw a janitor emptying trash cans, but there wasn't anybody else around.

They reached the third floor and made their way quietly down the hall to Rocco's office. Frank pushed the door open to reveal a man in a suit bent over in Professor Rocco's desk chair, carefully putting pieces of paper in the metal wastebasket next to the desk.

The man sat up and spun around in the chair to face the Hardys.

It was "Mr. Williams."

Chapter

14

WILLIAMS VAULTED THE DESK and went for the door, but Frank grabbed him and got him in an armlock. Williams pivoted away, though, with a textbook reversal that sent Frank skidding across the desk and onto the floor.

Frank pulled himself to his feet and saw Williams going after Joe. Joe raised a forearm to block a sweeping kick to his throat and then countered with a kick to the knee that sent Williams crashing to the floor. Williams slapped his palms down to absorb the impact and rolled back to his feet.

Joe still stood between the man and the door, and Frank moved to flank him. "Give it up," Frank said. "You're not getting past the two of us."

"Get out of my way," Williams snarled. He pulled a small black plastic device out of his coat pocket. Frank immediately realized it was a flash attachment for a camera, but before he could react, he was blinded by a flash of light.

Frank doubled over, clutching his eyes. All he could see was blackness punctuated by swimming silver blobs.

He heard a splintering of wood, a shout from Joe, and a heavy crash. Then the door slammed shut.

"Joe, are you okay?" Frank said.

"Well, that flash blinded me," Joe said. "Then he hit me with a chair. It feels as if someone parked a Volkswagen on my chest, but other than that I'm just great."

Frank's vision started to return, but it was like walking into a pitch-black room after being outside on a sunny day. He could see Joe pinned under the flipped-over desk. He went over and lifted up a corner so Joe could squirm out from under it.

"Thanks," Joe said as he got to his feet. He rubbed his arm where the chair had hit him. He knew there was going to be a bruise, but at least it wasn't broken. "Want to go after him?"

"What's the point?" Frank said. "He's long gone."

"So let's try to figure out what he was doing here," Joe said. He knelt down by the wastebasket and examined the papers that Williams had dropped into it. They were newspaper articles, torn up and partly burned.

"Why would he come back here as Rocco?" Joe asked, holding up a few large scraps. "Just to burn a few articles like this? He did a pretty crummy job of it, too. Look, you can still make out some of the dates and stuff."

"Not only did he do a crummy job," Frank said, kneeling next to his brother, "but he didn't do it here."

"What do you mean?"

"Everything in this can is cool. Also, do you smell any smoke? If he'd been burning stuff in here, there would be smoke."

"Right," Joe said. He started laying some of the fragments of newspaper out on the floor where they could both study them. "Why would he partly burn them somewhere else and then bring them here to throw them away?"

"Maybe they were supposed to be found," Frank said. "Maybe he wanted to make it look as if someone was destroying them."

Joe studied the articles. "Let's see. . . . We've got an article about Eli's kidnapping, one on the protests at the incinerator site. Here's part of a headline, 'Welcome . . .' "

"If Williams's plans had panned out," Frank said, "Eli would be dead and everybody would still think Williams was Professor Rocco. So it would look as if Professor Rocco had tried to burn these articles, right?"

"That's right," Joe said.

"Williams thinks the real Rocco is still on ice in Storage City," Frank said.

"Why on ice?" Joe asked.

"As Detective Loomis said, freezing makes it almost impossible to determine the time of death. Williams was in this office, leaving these newspaper articles to frame Professor Rocco, who would later turn up dead, while he walked away clean."

"Clean from what, though?" Joe asked. "He didn't go to all this trouble just to have a few bombs planted at the incinerator."

"No," Frank said. "But if we can reconstruct some of these articles, maybe we can figure out what he was trying to frame Rocco for. That could be the key."

Joe stared at the articles and shook his head. "There's not a lot here to work with."

They spread the fragments out on the desk and started fitting them together. It was like putting together a jigsaw puzzle with half of its pieces missing.

"Whatever he's up to," Joe said, "it has something to do with the general."

"Albright is definitely the focus," Frank said.

Joe connected two pieces of headline and slid them over next to the piece that began "Welcome . . ." He had the full headline now: "Welcome Back Bash at Baker's."

"It's about today's reception at the president's house," Joe said. "Albright is the guest of honor."

"Let's see," Frank said, pausing to think it through. "Williams would wait to plant these articles until he was almost ready to act, right? The reception is just getting started. All faculty members are invited. So Williams gets in, posing as Rocco."

"Frank, I just realized something," Joe said. "Remember the break-in?" he said, pointing to a snippet about the failed burglary at the university president's house.

"Yep," Frank said.

"Even if Williams gets in posing as Rocco, he couldn't sneak any kind of weapon past security. So he staged the break-in to plant the weapon he needs to use later."

"Williams is going after Albright," Frank said slowly.

"He's going to kill the general," Joe said.

"Unless we stop him," Frank answered.

Chapter

15

"LET'S MOVE OUT. Quick," Joe said.

The Hardys ran downstairs and hopped into their van. While Joe tried to get Officer De-Finis or Detective Loomis on the cell phone, Frank drove full-speed to the university president's house.

"Any luck?" Frank asked his brother as he accelerated to make a yellow light.

"No," Joe answered. "Loomis isn't at his desk. They're looking for Mike. I'm on hold."

He was still on hold when they pulled up to the president's estate. They drove straight past a line of cars parked along the U-shaped drive. Several plainclothes security men at the front door were checking invitations and directing guests through a metal detector shaped like a doorframe.

"A lot of good that's going to do," Joe muttered. He hung up the phone as Frank double-parked about twenty yards from the door.

"We don't have time to answer any questions," Frank said as they jumped out of the van. "Let's just crash this party and deal with the consequences later."

"You try to reach the general," Joe said. "I'll find Williams."

They cut to the front of the line where a man with a crew cut wearing a dark suit held out his hand and said, "Your invitations, please."

"No, thanks," Joe said, shouldering the man into his colleagues and charging through the metal detector. Frank followed Joe at a dead run. They heard somebody behind them shout, "Breach at the front door."

They shoved their way through the crowd of guests and burst into a foyer with a white marble floor and ferns in big pots. Two marines in full-dress uniform were standing guard. They lowered their rifles at Frank and Joe. Veering to the side, Joe grabbed one of the rifles by the barrel, yanked it away, and shoved the marine into his partner with it, knocking them both down.

As the rifle clattered to the floor, Frank and

Joe sidestepped the fallen marines and darted into a grand ballroom with a big buffet laid out to the right. The room was full of guests. At the far end of the buffet table was a draped platform with a lectern. General Albright was just mounting the steps.

Most of the crowd had its attention on the general, but Frank saw a pair of plainclothes security agents moving toward him. He would have to get past them to reach the general.

Frank ran toward the two agents, weaving among the guests. They didn't have their weapons drawn yet—obviously they knew better than to risk gunfire in such a crowded place—but they were closing in on Frank fast.

Frank used a move that had worked for him on a punt return during the past football season. He slowed down, faked left, and spun right. That got him past the agents, but now his path was blocked by a group of guests crowding the buffet table.

Frank glanced up and saw Mr. Williams standing on the hearth of a massive fireplace across the hall. In his hand was an automatic pistol. He had a clear shot at the general, who had paused on the platform steps. Frank could see Joe bulling his way through the crowd, but he might not get to Williams in time.

There was only one way for Frank to reach the general.

He vaulted onto the buffet table, landing between a pan of Swedish meatballs and a tray of crab puffs. He ran the length of the table, avoiding the appetizers but accidentally taking out a bowl of caviar and leaving a footprint in the chocolate mousse.

"Get down!" Frank yelled at the general, but he was drowned out by shouts and screams from the crowd.

Three bodyguards were poised at the bottom of the stairs between Frank and the general. Frank leaped off the end of the table and over the bodyguards, who were clutching at his legs. He managed to hit the general at the waist and take him down in a flying tackle.

Two gunshots rang out as Frank and the general fell, and two small craters appeared in the wall behind where the general had been standing.

Across the room Joe heard the gunshots at close range as he piled into Williams. The two of them fell to the marble floor, and the gun skidded off into the crowd. The assassin was on his feet again in a flash, but so was Joe.

"Come on," Joe said. "Just try me."

The assassin slumped his shoulders and held up his hands in surrender. Joe relaxed for a second, but as soon as he did, Williams launched a vicious kick at his head.

Joe was ready for it. He ducked under the

blow and countered with a sweeping low kick of his own that knocked Williams's feet out from under him. The stunned assassin started to get up again, but half a dozen agents were already on top of him, weapons drawn.

Meanwhile three more of them grabbed Joe and pinned him to the floor.

"All right, let the kid go," a stern voice said. Joe got up to see General Albright walking toward him. He was followed by Frank and several bodyguards.

Joe grinned at his brother, whose pant legs were splattered with food. "You know, Frank," he said. "It's really not considered polite to tap-dance on the buffet table at a reception.

Later the general sent a limousine to pick the Hardys and Richie up for dinner.

"At least they gave us a chance to get dressed this time," Joe commented on the way over.

They were ushered into the same hotel suite where they had eaten breakfast with General Albright.

"Welcome, gentlemen," the general said as he rose to greet them. "And thanks again for what you did this afternoon."

"Thanks for having us over, sir," Frank said.

"I figured I owed you a meal," the general

said as he shook Frank's hand, "especially since the buffet this afternoon lost a lot of its appeal when you stepped all over it."

Joe let out a guffaw. Frank had taken plenty of ribbing earlier when he spent an hour trying to get the chocolate stains out of his favorite pair of high-tops.

"Please, sit down," the general said. "From what I hear, you three have already figured out a good deal of the assassin's plot. I thought you might like to know the rest of the story."

"Did he talk?" Frank asked.

"He certainly did," the general said with a satisfied smile. "He worked out a deal. Your Mr. Williams turns out to be quite the world-renowned hit man. His real name is Alfred Travali. He's known as the Janitor because he specializes in cleaning up other people's messes—eliminating witnesses, nosy reporters, that sort of thing. He's wanted in at least fourteen countries around the world. Rather than have us extradite him someplace where they'd probably just stand him up and shoot him tomorrow at dawn, he agreed to tell us everything. Also, I think he enjoyed the chance to brag about his exploits."

"So who hired him?" Frank asked.

"I don't know how closely you boys follow current events," the general said, leaning back on the sofa, "but here's the basic idea. In the civil war in Gabiz, the current government is fighting against its own military. The government needed soldiers to fight the rebellious troops, so it hired mercenaries. They're the ones who stand to profit most from the war."

"So the mercenaries hired the Janitor to wipe you out," Joe said.

"Correct," the general replied. "Then the two sides would blame each other for my death, and the war would rage on. They hired the best assassin, because my security is extremely tight—especially when I'm in Gabiz, which is why he chose to strike here."

"Okay, so he killed Professor Rocco and took his place," Frank said. "And he was going to frame the professor and Eli for the assassination. But I can't figure out why he killed the professor and kept Eli alive."

"The professor's death was an accident," the general said. "After the assassination, the Janitor planned to escape in a small plane with the professor. He would bail out, the plane would crash, and the world would think the assassin—Professor Rocco—had been killed trying to slip out of the country. When he abducted Professor Rocco, he used a tricky choke hold and just held it too long. 'A simple miscalculation,' I think is how he put it."

Joe put his hand to his neck, feeling the bruise where the Janitor had choked him until he blacked out. "I'm familiar with that type of hold," Joe said. "It's definitely dangerous."

The general gave Joe a sympathetic smile and continued. "He froze Rocco's body so the coroner wouldn't be able to tell he had been dead before the crash and ruin his frame job. When Eli stumbled into his plans, he decided to frame them both. Eli was supposed to die in the plane crash, too."

A knock sounded at the door, and the general got up to greet two more guests—Jessica and Eli. The Hardys and Richie stood up to say hello. Frank thought they both looked smug.

"What's going on?" Frank said. "You two look as if somebody just gave you a million-dollar lottery ticket. What's the big secret?"

"It's no secret," the general said with a sigh as he sat down. "I guess you boys didn't listen to the evening news."

"Frank usually does, but he's been too busy cleaning his shoes," Joe said.

Jessica grinned. "Congress held an emergency session and voted to suspend the incinerator project," she said.

"Thanks to the efforts of a local student organization and its leader," the general said, "who used the publicity surrounding her father's visit to Langston University to get the people's ear. I may disagree with you on some of the issues, Jess, but I do admire your determination."

Jessica hugged him. "Thanks, Dad."

"Nothing like a near assassination to bring a family closer together," Richie murmured, earning him an elbow in the ribs from Frank.

The general put an arm around Eli's shoulders and squeezed. "And you, young man, I don't agree with you on the issues either, but I'm glad we're both alive to help Jessica celebrate."

"Me, too," Eli said. At first he seemed leery of the general's affection, but after a moment he relaxed.

"Now let's go eat," the general said, ushering them all toward the door. "And while we're at dinner, maybe the rest of us Langston people can talk Frank and Joe into enrolling."

Frank and Joe looked at each other and shook their heads.

"I don't think we're ready for this place," Frank said.

"Too much excitement," Joe said. "We'd never make it to class."

Frank and Joe's next case:

Frank and Joe are headed out on a Kentucky spelunking expedition—exploring caves, that is. But on this particular descent, something stinks to high heaven. Joe stumbles onto an uncharted subcavern, and suddenly the entire expedition is under attack. Apparently Joe went too far, saw too much, and his curiosity could prove fatal.

The deeper the boys look into the cave, the more hazardous to their health it becomes. They're attacked by a murderous fellow explorer, snared in an ancient booby trap, and caught in a vicious whirlpool. But the Hardys are not about to back down. They're determined to unearth the deadly secret hidden in the cave—even if their search takes them to the very bottom of a chasm of danger ... in *Cave Trap,* Case #115 in The Hardy Boys Casefiles™.

Christopher Pike presents....
a frighteningly fun new series for your younger brothers and sisters!

SPOOKSVILLE

The Secret Path 53725-3/$3.50
The Howling Ghost 53726-1/$3.50
The Haunted Cave 53727-X/$3.50
Aliens in the Sky 53728-8/$3.99
The Cold People 55064-0/$3.99
The Witch's Revenge 55065-9/$3.99
The Dark Corner 55066-7/$3.99
The Little People 55067-5/$3.99
The Wishing Stone 55068-3/$3.99
The Wicked Cat 55069-1/$3.99
The Deadly Past 55072-1/$3.99

A MINSTREL BOOK